ROSEMARY OKAFOR

ONE MORE NIGHT

First Published in Great Britain in 2020 by
LOVE AFRICA PRESS
103 Reaver House, 12 East Street, Epsom KT17 1HX
www.loveafricapress.com

ISBN: 978-1-914226-02-1
Also available as ebook

DEDICATION

To David, my husband, with love.

ACKNOWLEDGMENTS

More than dozens of African Romance and Chic-lit writers have probably thanked Kiru Taye for making their voices heard. Here is me adding my own "Thank you" to this woman who took a chance with me. And to Zee Monodee a superb editor, she owns this work in a unique way only the two of us understand. And finally my first Creative writing teacher, Titi Awobode, thank you so much, my instructor-turn-sister.

BLURB

A night with Grace's ex husband reignites old feelings she thought long buried and provides a second chance for her dead marriage. With a world of uncertainty between them, they must determine if the reasons that tore them apart in the first place will do so again.

Imelda has known one kind of love—hard, stressful and abusive. Then she crosses paths with Kolawole, a far cry from her usual taste in men. With an old debt to pay, forced loyalty and blackmail, can she walk away from an old relationship that threatens to tear her apart?

Chinyeaka's life has not been easy. But she's determined to get the future she deserves by any means necessary.

One More Night weaves the stories of these women as they search for love, second chances, forgiveness and self rediscovery.

CHAPTER ONE

Kenneth Ojukwu opened the door on the second knock. He wasn't expecting her, not today, not anytime soon. The last time she'd visited had been two months ago, and it had left him miserable.

"This is the last time I will come to your house."

Now she stood there, drenched. Stray locks of hair curled across her forehead and her temples.

"Can I come in?" she asked.

"Yes, sure."

What else could he say?

She walked past him into the sitting room. His gaze swept over her curves and rested on her backside. Thanks to the rain, her short gown which clung to her body left little or nothing from the eyes.

"Sorry to bother you by this time. My tire went bad, and I couldn't get someone to help me out before it started raining." She blew into her cupped hands and rubbed them. "By the time it was fixed, it was already late," she said through chattering teeth. "You know how terrible I am when it comes to driving at night." Her eyes followed his gaze over her body. "I don't have an umbrella." She shrugged and chuckled nervously. "But if you don't want me, I can leave—"

"Oh, no, no … You don't have to go anywhere," he interrupted, rubbing his sweaty palm on his shirt. "It's okay with me." He scratched his jaw. "Please go to the bathroom and change into something dry. You can make do with any of my old shirts. I hope you can still find your way around?"

"Yes, that is if you have not changed a lot of things," she said, flashing him a warm smile.

Desire smouldered in him as he watched her climb the stairs. Grace … Their marriage would have been seven years long if she hadn't walked away. She was his pride—his friends used to tell him how lucky he was to marry such an enigma. Who could ever believe that they would not make it to their fourth wedding anniversary?

She turned and caught him staring. He quickly looked away.

"Ehm … I will go check if there is anything left in the kitchen," he stuttered before she entered the guest room and closed the door behind her.

This was not the first time she was showing up on his doorstep after their separation. It was bliss the first year of marriage until their incompatibility became loud, and they realized they could not go on. She was a career-driven woman while he was a family guy.

They'd talked, dialogued, lost tempers, accused each other, had heated arguments about her preference for her job and how he wasn't supportive, how they needed space to sort themselves out.

But she kept coming over to the house. Either to take a piece of clothing she'd left behind or to pick up a document that belonged to her firm. The last time, she'd said she wanted to check on him, and today, she had come to tempt him, with that thing she wore! After this long, his hormones still responded to the attractive woman that was once his wife.

"Can I help with the coffee?" came the sultry voice behind him.

His response caught in his throat as he turned. His old shirt hung loose on her body with nothing underneath, her nipples visible through the fabric.

"Uh … hope what I put on is okay with you?" she asked, following his gaze.

"Yes ... yes, don't mind me. I have not seen you in those for a long time." Desire washed through him, and he swallowed.

"So can I help with the coffee?" she asked again.

"Sure. Just come over here and help me with the coffee maker."

She was too close for comfort; they kept brushing against each other. Having her in the kitchen was a mistake. He was about to get some eggs from the fridge when they collided.

"I am so sorry." She chuckled. "The cold is making me clumsy."

He wasn't listening. With his hands around her waist and her breasts brushing against his chest, he burned with need.

They held each other's gaze for a while, breaths coming faster, hearts throbbing, her lips parted, her eyes longing, her scent intoxicating.

He bent his head. Lips touched lips. Hers opened more, and he got lost in them. He took what she offered like a hungry man in need of food. As he drew her closer, his hands strayed a little here and there.

They were brought back from the world of ecstasy by the whistling of the kettle.

"We shouldn't be doing this," he said.

"We are supposed to be divorced," she giggled and replied.

"Babe, we can still remarry. Just move in with me. Let's stop this madness," he pleaded.

"Kay …" She shut her eyes and shook her head. "You know how it is. We cannot work as a couple."

And there it came … Ken gave her a hard stare, released his hold on her arms. "Let's eat."

Neither brought up the incident. Nonetheless, the memory hung over them as they ate.

*

Ken sat at the dining table, stock cards and invoices spread before him, his laptop on. Grace coming in to set his emotions on turmoil had kept him awake the night before, yet he couldn't get his mind together to work this morning!

Last night was one of those when his eyes denied him sleep. Torture—that's what she did to him.

Her beautiful hips, what she did with her waist while walking into the room, leaving him drooling—was that deliberate? Her sensual lips, her nipples taut and visible in the shirt, daring him to run his fingers on them, give then sensual bites, chastise her for all the nights he had dreamt of them, to make her scream in pleasure like she used to, and in pain for punishing him with her subtle bodily manipulation …

"Grace," he muttered. "We would have made this work."

"I did not know you had upgraded from manual stock-taking and accounting to digital."

Her voice jolted him out of the nostalgia. She was already dressed, hair neatly packed up above her neck, and her lips glowed with red lipstick.

"And I didn't know you now wear extensions and lipstick," he said with a mixture of surprise and amusement.

"I grew up, matured, you old-fashioned Igbo man." She laughed.

"Well, this old-fashioned Igbo man has also grown. I have learned how to use 'pitch tree' for my digital accounting," he boasted.

Both of them burst into hearty laughter, followed by an awkward silence.

"Uh … I have to start going now … before, uh … Mary notices that I am still here," Grace stuttered, avoiding his eye.

"Won't you have breakfast? I can fix you something quick." He wanted her to stay little more.

"No, Kay, I don't want the neighbours to see me here, especially Mary. She will start a gossip."

He gave a bitter smile. She is still the same, alright, cares more about what others would say about her than how I feel.

"Okay, have a great day at the office," he said.

CHAPTER TWO

"You are late," Mary chattered as Grace pulled out files and papers. "The investors from Grandville are already here, the boss asked you to see him immediately after you come in, and … I saw your car parked in front of Ken's house on my way to work. Girlfriend, are you getting your groove on without letting me know?"

"Oh my, I'm roasted," Grace swore under her breath, then dialled her secretary. "Imelda, please help me with the last month's company promotion sales records. I can't find it in my system," she said at the young lady that walked in immediately.

"Okay, ma'am," Imelda replied.

"Is the conference room ready for the presentation?" she asked.

"Mr. Oluwale is on it, ma'am."

"Wow, wait a minute! Are you, like, giving me the 'ignore the chatterbox' treatment?" Mary cut in. "See, oh girl, you owe me this gist. You are not escaping. You are giving me this gist 'hot hot' even if it means squeezing it out of your mouth."

Mary stood there, barricading the entrance to the office.

Grace was laughing now.

"Okay, Mary. What do you want to know?" she asked with a sigh.

"First, what was your car doing in front of Ken's apartment this morning? Secondly, did you sleep at his place? Thirdly, how long has this been going on, and fourth—"

"Slow down, girl! Jesus! Your amebo antenna is already on a high frequency this morning," Grace cut in.

"Grace Onwuka!" her boss shouted from the hall.

"Coming, sir" she called back. She meandered her way past Mary's bulky frame and out of the office. "See you later, girlfriend. Duty calls."

"I knew you had some before coming. I could perceive it all over you," Mary whispered.

"Get out of here ... tatafo republic," Grace responded as she walked down the hall.

"Was it super sweet?" Mary shouted back at her.

"I don't know what you are talking about!" she threw back amidst chuckles.

*

The applause was resounding.

"Congratulations, Mr Ogungbeso. We are convinced your company will not let us down." Chief Okwudili, Managing Director of Sanchez Bank, shook hands with the MD of the New Breed Advertising and Promotion Company.

"Oh, not at all, sir. We have the best brains around, and we will give your company an image that is second to none in this country," Mr Ogungbeso replied, beaming with smiles.

"I hope so, friend. Ehem ... Talking about 'best brains,' that lady that handled this presentation, she sure knows her onion in this job, the kind of brain I love working with." Chief grabbed his satchel from the polished mahogany desk.

"No, Chief, don't go there. We are not letting her go soon," Mr Ogungbeso said.

"Don't worry, my friend. I'm not ready to charm her yet." They both laughed. "I'm going over to have a chat."

Grace couldn't contain her joy, and her heart jittered. She'd done it again! She'd wowed the clients, and going by the resounding applause, the papers and pens changing hands, her company had gotten the one-year contract to promote Sanchez Bank on radio, TV, and other social media platforms.

"Young lady, you hypnotized all of us today with your level of intelligence." Chief Okwudili shook her hand with admiration. "Here is my card. Don't forget to call me if this man does not give you a raise for this," he joked.

"That's nice of you, sir," she replied.

"See me in my office before you leave today, Grace," her boss said over his shoulder on his way out with the client.

The leather chair squeaked as she collapsed on it. She was not in a hurry to go back to her office, not to meet Mary and her many questions about last night.

Last night ...

They had been close to ripping their clothes off and making out on the kitchen floor. Perfect for each other—sex between them had always been breath-taking.

She threw her head backwards and exhaled as she recalled memories of how it used to be between them. Passionate, and last night, she'd realised she still lost her sanity at his touch. Once, she had dared to imagine another woman in his arms; the thought had stung her with jealousy, though.

Is that why I keep going to him?

She couldn't deny the fact that she wanted him so much and wouldn't have minded that kitchen floor, by the way. She had desired to be held in his arms, to rub her fingers on his head and spank his naked butt as he rode her senseless. She'd wanted his tongue down her wetness while she held his head.

The thought triggered a shiver. "Ahrrr …"

She could feel the tingling between her legs, this sensation that made her throw her head backwards and lick her lips as she imagined him doing those beautiful sexual things to her …

"Kay …" she muttered, rubbing her hands around her shoulders.

Ken was one crazy lover who was not ashamed of making out anywhere at any time.

"Where did you come from?" she had asked once.

"If you desire someone, you cannot keep your hands to yourself, and you, my wife, are very desirable."

He could grab her ass and brush her breast anywhere. Nasty in a beautiful way. She'd gotten used to him, and always dreamed of those moments. Until her work started demanding more while Ken got freer from his. He got more people to handle sales and branch offices, and she … She started staying late at work, from one meeting to another; she travelled more often, and Ken began to complain. He had understood at first—or so she'd thought, but on their third year of marriage, he could no longer cope with her many travels. They'd drifted so far apart.

Coming together was no longer an option.

"Here you are." Mary playfully slammed her hand on the table. "You think you can run away from me?" She pulled a chair and sat. "Babe! I heard you nailed it, as usual!"

Both laughed happily.

"I overheard the boss talking about giving you a raise." Mary had lowered her voice.

"Wow! Are you serious?" Grace had actually been expecting this news.

"Of course, he has no choice." Mary took a bottle of water from the conference table, unscrewed it, and gulped back. "Anyways, lunch is on you today. Let's go," she said, dragging Grace along.

CHAPTER THREE

"So, girlfriend, if I am getting what you just explained, your showing up at Ken's doorstep wasn't anything but a call for help. You are not secretly screwing him, and you have no plan of doing so. Your life is more boring than mine," Mary said dramatically over lunch.

"That's not fair, Mary. I'm not that boring. Besides, I don't think I have the time to go on a seduction mission," Grace replied with a full mouth.

"Gracie, Gracie!" Mama Obafemi came over to their table. "Make I bring another meat for you na, I get better goat meat, wey get correct pepper inside," she said, grinning at the two of them.

Mama Obafemi Restaurant had been their favourite spot for lunch, for at least four years now. It was not just a place for delicious lunches, but one for letting their guards down and gossip.

"Ra ra, Ma," she said, indicating no in Yoruba. "Your food is delicious as usual, but I can't eat more than this," she politely replied.

"Ehm ... Iya, I will take that goat meat. Put it in a takeaway plate for me. Gracie will pay," Mary cut in towards Mama.

"Oda' I go bring am now now," a happy Mama Obafemi replied then disappeared into her kitchen.

"How did I become close to you!" Grace jokingly screamed at Mary.

"Ask yourself!"

"What do I do with you, Mary?"

"Pay for the food and my take away," her friend replied, and they both laughed.

"So, how is Mami?" Mary asked while wiping her mouth with a serviette.

"My mum is there o. I dread calling her these days. She would remind me that I'm working too much, I need a break so I can make my marriage work again and give her grandchildren ... Mtcheeeewww, I can't deal with her anymore."

"She doesn't know you guys are already divorced?"

"She does, but she still nurses the hope that Ken and I will get back together."

"Please allow the poor woman to keep her hope alive joor. Anyways, I still agree with her that you need a vacation. Babe, you have been working too hard. For these few months, I have watched you wipe out fun from your life, and you have buried yourself in building another man's company," Mary admonished.

"Mary, I'm building myself. This is who I am now. I can't change it. Please don't make me feel miserable."

CHAPTER FOUR

Grace had seen him a few minutes ago, haggling with a market woman. His back to her, she took painful pleasure at looking him over. He had gone all bald—she'd noticed the last time she had visited—and it gave him a sharp masculine look. His shoulders looked broader, too.

She flushed. She should be ashamed of herself, thinking of those strong arms stroking her, at the market, in a meat shop.

He glanced over his shoulder and met her stare. Her breath caught sharply, and she looked away without a second glance. He would come to her, no doubt. Ken wasn't one to turn away whenever he set his eyes on her. She swallowed hard, heart racing, and forced her concentration on the meat seller.

"My Madam, Bawo," Suleman greeted.

"Sule, how are you?" she replied.

"I dey o Madam, na only bad market dey worry me," he complained.

"Don't worry, Sule, customers are co—"

She had been about to finish her statement when a familiar voice interrupted her.

"The best thing about buying meat in the open market is that you get the chance to flip it front and back and give it close scrutiny." That was what he'd said to her the first time he'd brought her to this place. "So you still come to this market?"

His smile flooded her with warmth.

"Ken! What are you doing here?" She smiled back.

One look on those moist wide brown eyes and she was fighting the urge to rush into his arms. He had that effect on her—since the day he'd barricaded and seduced her into giving him her phone number.

"The same thing you are doing here," he replied, and they both laughed.

"So, who cooks for you now? I don't see any lady by your side, or is she waiting at home?"

It shouldn't bother her anymore, yet the thought of another woman in his house tightened her chest.

"Oh, Grace, you hurt me now." Ken faked sadness. "You have forgotten I used to cook for you."

She remembered. He was a perfect cook and had enjoyed cooking for them. "Don't mind me, Ken. I was only pulling your leg."

"I thought you wanted to know if I have ladies coming around the house to do things for me ..."

He had a glint in his eyes! He was reading her like a book and had sensed her jealousy.

"Oh, no, Ken. Please, you are free to do anything you want. Just be safe."

She picked her meat from Suleman. She would not allow him to see how weak he made her. Her brick wall gave way when she faced him again—he was staring and smiling! He knew the effect he had on her.

"I will seduce you back to me," he had said three nights ago.

But seduction didn't build a marriage.

"Seriously, Kay ... it really doesn't matter what you do with your life now." She bit her lip as the words left her mouth.

He frowned. "I thought you would be worried if I had told you that some lady does come around the house. I forgot you have moved on."

No, Kay. It had been difficult moving on with him always in her mind. The longing, desire, jealousy each time she thought of him with another lady. "I have not moved on!" she wanted to scream.

"I just want you to be free … ehm … you know …" she stammered and shrugged.

"You don't have to explain anything, Grace." He masked his disappointment with a smile. "I am making 'Ofe Akwu' tomorrow. You can come over the house and have a taste of real food," he joked.

"I don't know … but I will try. I'm salivating already." She joined him in laughing.

But deep in her heart, as much as she would want to even spend forever with him, there remained an unsettled edge between them. With the circumstances that had led to their divorce, heightening their feelings for each other wouldn't help them. Coming together in his house would not help her forget him.

*

It's just a regular visit.

Yet, she was indecisive about what to wear. The contents in her wardrobe had relocated to her bed as she has been changing clothes, but none fitted.

"It's just a normal visit," she repeated to herself for the umpteenth time, but she secretly desired to have him look at her and lick his lips. "What is wrong with me?" she said under her breath.

She finally settled for the simple, sleeveless and sequined, short red gown she'd bought last Easter, with silver stud earrings and silver opened-toe shoes to go with the outfit. She was just putting the final touch of makeup on her face when her phone rang.

"Hi." His voice filtered through.

"Hi." She held her breath.

He did not speak for some seconds, then, "Ehm … I just want to know if you are alright."

"Yes," she said, almost choking. "Yes, I am," she added more clearly.

A few minutes later, she was seated quietly in the cab questioning her sanity and wondering if Ken still found her attractive.

What was it that had made her walk away that night? Guilt? Shame? Pity? She had been on the verge of being promoted for the second time in a year while getting ready for her wedding to Ken—she remembered what her MD had told her the day she'd given him her letter of invitation.

"You have to work extra hard for promotions and increase, now that you are getting married. You know marriage has a way of slowing women down."

She hated how Mary had remained an executive marketer. Three years after her marriage, she kept fronting kids and marital status as an excuse for her incompetence, took more days off, and would report to work late with 'sick children' as the explanations. Grace also hated the fact that Mary's husband seemed to control her life—Mary would be the first to leave the office after work, bringing her husband into every conversation, including official ones. She had watched Mary lose her passion and settle into family life and motherhood.

Grace had vowed not to end up like Mary, or her mother, who'd had the chance of becoming the Local Government Chairman in 1993. Grace had been ten years old then, had seen her parents argue a lot, her father screaming at her mother each time she came home late from those party meetings.

"How could you abandon these kids for some useless politics? Have you forgotten you are a woman? Your primary assignment lies with these children," her father would say to her mum.

"I told Nwamaka to look after them." Her mother would try to defend herself.

"What would Nwamaka do? Would Nwamaka breastfeed Ekenedilichukwu, your eight-month-old son?"

Her father had summoned her mother's kinsmen. Grace had later learnt that her mother had been given the option of abandoning her political career to put her home in order or forgetting the marriage entirely.

Her mother had chosen to stay with them but was never happy. She seized every moment alone with them to lament about how unfair she was judged.

"I would have been better off a single woman," she would say. "He is threatened by my political success."

Her mother had been sceptical about Ken, but Grace had assured her that Ken was not just educated but also the son of a woman who was once the Vice-Chancellor of a university. "He knows I love my job."

"Wasn't your father a PhD holder, yet he killed my political dreams?" her mother had argued.

But she'd felt Ken understood her love for her job. A month to their wedding, she'd raised the issue of waiting a few years before having babies, and Ken had vehemently objected to it.

"Children are one of the spices of marriage. Why should we delay having them?" he'd said.

She'd known she was in trouble. She couldn't start having children immediately—she wanted to secure her place as the Head of Advertising and Promotions first and prove her worthiness for the position before she would settle down into motherhood.

The driver tooted the horn as he navigated his way out of the gridlock that had become part of Abebi Road, into Toyin Street.

The house came into view. This used to be her home. She could remember the pride in Ken's eyes the day he'd brought her to that house for the first time. It had been her birthday, and he'd wanted to surprise her.

"Four rooms? What do we need four rooms for?" she had asked.

"Our daughter will have that room close to ours. That is why I painted it pink. One for us, and the remaining two will be for our two sons." He had been grinning all over.

As the cab pulled up in front of the gate, she looked at the house again, and the memory of last time came calling, the intense sexual attraction and her longing for him. She doubted her comportment and self-control with Ken.

"I am here already. It's just a harmless date," she said under her breath.

"Were you talking to me, ma'am?" the cab driver called back.

"Oh, no … Here is your money. I will call you when I'm ready to leave."

*

Useless.

Wasn't he trying too hard? She had made it clear she no longer wanted them together. He threw his phone on the sofa, slid the window open, and peered out. He was too old for this. At forty-two, he wasn't supposed to be waiting for a lady like a boy on his first date.

She isn't any lady.

She was his little lady.

His heart sank. "I should have known she was not coming."

He dropped the curtain and sagged against the wall. Like always, she had proven to him that she had a mind of her own and couldn't be talked into making compromises. He hissed and walked towards the kitchen, opened the pot of rice, and got a plate to serve himself.

The doorbell rang. He ignored it at first, picked up the serving spoon, but the persisting pealing made him drop the plate and stride to the door.

He stiffened. She was there—she had come! Shivering all over, he felt like lifting her up and swinging her around in his joy.

"Are you going to keep me standing here?" she asked, her face beaming.

CHAPTER FIVE

"Why did you do it?"

Ken finally asked the question that had been in his heart like a stone, the confusion hanging on his mind like a heavy weight on the neck of a bull. He hadn't planned to bring it up. They had flirted with each other over dinner—when was the last time he'd had so much fun in a few hours?

"Dinner was great," she had told him with excitement.

"I am glad you finally made it. I thought you wouldn't come," he had replied, excitement vibrating in his voice.

It had been so long since they'd eaten together like this, and it seemed like ages since he'd seen her cute face light up with excitement after a meal. She was a foodie; he loved that, among other things, about her.

He had drowned in her charm, the gleam in her eyes when she laughed. But she was right—lust alone wouldn't hold them together no matter how much they craved each other. They had to talk about it. He deserved an answer.

"I have tried to get you back all these years, and you have told me one thing—that desire is not enough." He fiddled with his ring; he couldn't let it go, too, and today, he had noticed she still had hers. "You are right, Grace. You never gave me any reason why you did what you did to us. Rather, you chose to walk away." He crossed his hands on his chest, leaned against the fridge. "Grace, why did you do it?"

Shoulders stiff, she did not turn to look at him, nor did she say a word as she scrubbed the plates harder.

"Why did you prevent us from having at least a child?" he asked again, this time louder.

She hadn't explained the first time he'd asked—the night he'd read her text message and discovered she had an IUCD.

'My flow has become very heavy after this implant. Is it normal?' the text had read.

She had come out of the bathroom to see him with the phone.

Beads of perspirations had formed on his forehead.

"Grace!" he had whispered in horror and disbelief. "All these years, we have prayed together, asking God for a baby!"

She had stood there, her blue towel wrapped loosely around her, mouth tight.

He had grabbed his shirt and left. She wasn't there when he got back, had left him a simple note saying, 'I'm sorry for being so foolish, I don't deserve you.'

She had run out instead of talking things over. Run! Like she was doing today.

And now, she was also ignoring him. He tightened his fist and heaved. He didn't understand what she was hiding. Why it was so heavy for her to talk about it?

"I … I don't know," she finally answered, back still to him. "I don't know, Ken," she added louder, facing him now.

He gripped her shoulder, fingers digging into her flesh.

"I deserve an explanation, Grace. You couldn't give me an answer then, and you are not giving any answer now. I need to know why, for Christ's sake! Was it my fault? Was it what I did? Come on, let's talk about it!" he shouted.

"I don't know, Ken! I was foolish and selfish. I couldn't face myself or you."

"I called you, Grace, but you did not pick my calls. I sent messages, and you did not reply. You sent your lawyer to me a month later with a flimsy paper. What was that supposed to explain?"

"I did what was best for us at the moment, Ken."

He threw his hands up and rolled his eyes. "Us! Really, Grace? It was never about us. I didn't even know what propelled you. As far as I know, you did what was best for you, Grace!"

"You needed a woman that will be there for you, give you all the children." Her eyes searched his face, tears coming down now. "I wasn't that woman."

Ken battled the urge to scream at her.

"I did not pick your calls because I did not know what to say to you. I was due for another promotion, and the position was too tasking that getting pregnant at the moment would have placed me at the losing end."

"You chose to delay pregnancy while making me believe we were just not lucky. You subjected us to different tests," he said coldly.

She nodded. "I realize how stupid I was later. I don't deserve to be married, not to a man like you."

She lowered her gaze.

"Did you get the promotion?" he finally asked.

She looked at him sharply.

"Did you?" he asked again.

"Yes."

"At least you got what you wanted. Congratulations." He sighed and walked out of the kitchen.

*

"Ashawooooo! Oloriburuku Radarada, Oloshi!"

Imelda was amused. "Typical quarrel between women."

"Yes o Auntie, this place is one day another drama," the Mallam selling suya to her replied.

"She is pretending like didn't hear me!" the voice continued, this time closer to her.

"Auntie, it's like this woman is talking to you o," the Mallam said to her.

"Agba iya! I am talking to you." The woman who owned the voice roughly pushed Imelda.

A glance at the woman told her that, whoever she was, she was ready to fight her.

"Madam, what did I do to you now?" Imelda asked, head slightly flinched back.

"Ah! You are asking me question? See this husband snatcher o!" The woman beckoned to everyone who cared to gather round. "Ewo! You don't know me o! You are fucking my husband, spending his money! I will kill you o … Wo` ma pa e o!" She clapped with every word.

"Jesus! I don't know this woman o. Madam, you are embarrassing—" Imelda shouted, her eyes darting around seeking aid.

"Thunder fire that your mouth Idiot, Oponu, Ole! Thieffffuuuu! Why will you know me? When you will be opening your legs for my husband, your boss! You don't know he has a wife?" the woman continued amidst cheers and boos of the crowd.

She held Imelda by her top, ripping the flimsy thing, and went for her bra, but was stopped by some spectators.

"Iwo' I will deal with you in this Lagos." The woman poked her finger into Imelda's face.

Imelda held her half-torn bra, desperately looking for an escape route. She didn't know how she would wriggle herself from the scene.

"Hop in!"

Finally, a messiah!

It was when they had driven away from the scene that she noticed her bag has been stolen.

Later, clutching an oversized coat, she stepped towards home. The good man who'd brought her had offered it to her.

"I can't take this." She had looked from the coat to the shy-looking, plump messiah.

His brow had burrowed. "You have nothing left of your clothes."

She didn't know how to explain the coat to Ahmad who would definitely ask who it belonged to, but she couldn't get herself to tell him that. "How do I get it back to you?"

He had scratched his beard, hesitated. "I don't know. I can call you to tell you how to get it across to me."

Fair enough, though she didn't know how it would be possible to see him again. She had alighted three yards away from hers, slightly hiding her face as she entered her house.

He didn't notice her, eyes glued to the television, leaning forward to get a better view of whatever he was watching. Not even the strong masculine scent from the coat made him turn his head.

She stood, gaze combing the sitting room. The empty cup he'd used for tea in the morning before she'd left for work was still on top of the table, and the plate that had once contained toasted bread now held cigarette ashes. She wiggled her nose as the stench from him slapped her in the face while she bent to gather the cup, the plate, and his boxers which he'd discarded in the heat of their passion last night, and walked out.

"Who was that man that dropped you off?"

Imelda jerked her head as she stepped out of the bathroom to meet his cold gaze. He was not supposed to have seen her. Her eyes went to her box, where she had hidden the coat. He had his back against the door, hands folded across his chest.

Not today, please. Her body would not be able to take any pain, not when she still hurt from the beating last night. She took her nightgown from the wardrobe, ignoring him.

They'd graduated together from the university. While she was quick to get a job, Ahmad wasn't that lucky. He was jobless for three years before she got him a job through a friend in a surveying company, a position he lost four months after.

"Am I not asking you a question? Who was the Ogbeni that dropped you off?" he bellowed.

"He … he is just someone that gave me a lift." She backed away as he approached her.

"Just someone that gave you a lift, you say? As in what na? As a queen Elizabeth that you are na abi?" He sneered.

"Ahmad, please, I am not ready for this right now. I had a terrible day and—"

"Are you mad? You telling me you have a terrible day … are you insane?"

He charged towards her, gave her a slap, and pushed her to the bed. Her towel went loose, and he pulled his belt. Every lash followed with a derogatory and demeaning word. When she thought it was over, he unzipped his trousers and decided to pay himself for a job well done.

"Ahmad, what are you doing? Ahmad, please don't do this … Please I'm begging you, please stop …" she cried.

He paid her no ear, thrust like he was lashing her. They had had sex severally after many fights, but he had never raped her before, never used her in her pains. He always apologised, showing how sorry he was with passionate sex.

"Is this not what you went to do with the man? Because he has a car and I don't? He fucked you, and you enjoyed it." He was thrusting deeper and faster. "Are you not enjoying my fuck? Wasn't it what you want from him?"

He ejaculated, climbed down, and gave her a quick glance. For a second, Imelda thought she saw remorse written all over him, but it was soon masked with his deflected pride.

He took his trousers and walked out of the room.

*

Grace woke up on Sunday with a thud and the memory of yesterday's visit in her head. She had left his house with her eyes blinded by tears. He had not made any effort to stop her. She'd been so lost in her sorrow, she hadn't known when the driver had pulled over in front of her apartment.

"Excuse me, ma'am … Ma'am … We are here."

She had given him a nod and two thousand Naira. She'd flung herself on her sofa immediately after she'd opened her door and cried herself to sleep. She'd known a day like that would come—she had dreaded the moment she would look him in the face and tell him the truth.

She heaved herself off the sofa and staggered into her room before her phone rang.

"Good morning, Mom," she greeted strenuously.

"Ehen, how are you, Grace?"

"I'm doing well, Mom." She sniffed.

"You don't sound well. Are you sick?"

"No ... Not at all, Mom. I am just waking up, and I have been working too much lately."

"Okay, if you say so, though I'm not comfortable. Anyway ... hope you are still coming today?"

"Ah!" she exclaimed. "I totally forgot. Okay, let me try."

"Mba kwa! No, you will not try, you will come down here in the next one hour. Who do you want me to give all the food I painstakingly made for you?"

"I said I will try, Mom," she said again.

"When was the last time you visited me? Has your father's house become strange to you?"

"Mama, I said I will come. Don't start shouting yet," she assured her mother.

"That's better. See you in the next couple of hours," her mother replied with finality, and the phone went dead.

Always trying to control everybody's life. Grace sighed, grabbed her towel, and marched into the bathroom. She had once angrily called her mother a control freak, when she was trying to push her brother, Ekenedilichukwu, into changing from Theater Arts to Marine Engineering, two years after Ekene gained admission into the university. It took the intervention of family members for her to let the boy be.

What would happen if she chose not to honour her mother's invitation? Not that they were too fond of each other. After the death of her father, it had been challenging to stay under the same roof with her mother, who became unbearable, consumed with grief and guilt. School was an escape, and she had never wanted to return once she had tasted freedom.

She ruffled her hair while blow-drying, then left the hand dryer on her little dressing table and went for her clothes. She knew why her mother would want to see her. "What are you doing about your marriage? Do not make the same mistake I made," she would ask.

Like they have not discussed this over the phone severally that it was beginning to give her nightmares.

One more time, she told herself.

CHAPTER SIX

"What you need, gentlemen and ladies, is a promotion that will bring your company back into the minds of consumers," Chuka said.

"And how do you intend to achieve that?" Face tightened, Mr Morgan Cookey, the Chairman of the board of directors, relaxed his back on his office chair, massaged his temple, and asked.

"Re-branding, sir. Some of the beverages need to be re-branded," Grace came in, saving her junior colleague who was folding and unfolding his arms.

"Young lady, explain what you mean. We are not here for your grammar," another board member said impatiently.

"A change from bottles to attractive plastic containers, and a change in the label," she continued.

"And how do we push it back to the market?"

"That is where we come in, sir. We have a competent advertising team that can come out with a perfect advert. We can talk to some of the celebrities in the movie and music industry since these guys already have large followership on social media. Featuring them in the advert and making one or two of them brand ambassadors will be an advantage," she explained.

"These guys are not cheap. We are already losing money, and we can't risk the little money we have on paying celebrities for advertisement," a board member put in.

"Giving a company a business lift does not come cheap, sir." Chuka cast an angry look at the board member. "Besides, we can bargain with these guys. You are not paying them upfront. Business is a risk, gentlemen and ladies, which you should be willing to take."

"That is if it's worth it," someone interjected.

"You may not know how good a venture is unless you try. Your company is a household name, you are only having this problem with a product, and we need to get it back to the market. Won't you do anything to achieve that?" Grace asked.

They were silent for a while, then came a murmured agreement between the board members before the Chairman spoke.

"Okay, young lady, you have succeeded in convincing the board members to give this a try," he said.

"Thank you so much, sir." She was expecting this—never lost a deal. Wasn't it why she still had her job?

"But ... If this fails, I will not hesitate to have your head. Tell your boss I said so," the Chairman added.

"We will not fail you, sir," Grace said amidst a chuckle.

"Thank you, gentlemen and ladies. We can now retire for the day," the Chairman addressed his board members.

"Lady, please follow me to my office to sign some papers," he said to Grace.

She followed him, Chuka staying in the hallway.

"Your boss told me you can pull this off for us." Mr Cookey pushed the door that ushered them into his heavily furnished office. "I now know why. You are a very brilliant young girl ... And beautiful, too."

Grace frowned. 'Young girl!' What a condescending word to use on someone he was meeting for the first time. She was thirty-two, a mature woman. She didn't look anything like a girl.

But Ken has been using a similar word—little woman, her mind reminded her. Yet, that was different.

"Thank you, sir. I'm trying my best."

"Drop the 'Sir' and call me Morgan. We can be friends, you know." Without a glance in her direction, he pulled out some papers from a file on his table, took out his pen from his breast pocket, and scribbled his signature on three different documents. "You can take them with you if you want to study them before signing, but you and your team should get to work as soon as possible."

He finally cast his eyes on her, staring longer than he should. When he offered the papers, he was reluctant to let go.

"I like you," he blurted.

Grace cleared her throat and slipped the papers from his hands.

"Sure, sir, we will get to work immediately." She held his gaze, ignoring his last comment. "I hope I can take my leave now, sir."

"Yes, sure." Mr Cookey stood, walked around his desk to where she stood. Resting his butt against the wood, his hands supporting his weight, he leered at her. "Dinner anytime?"

"I don't think so, Sir. I really don't like going out late," she said, laughing uncomfortably.

"Come on, it's a harmless dinner, and besides, I already said I like you." He kept on observing her.

"I appreciate that, sir, but I am ... uh ... married." She nearly choked, fresh guilt hitting her like a rock.

"Don't deceive yourself, Grace. I know you are divorced," he blurted. "See, you need a powerful man like me in your life. You are divorced, and I am a widower. We can help each other."

Her phone rang, and relief washed over her. "Sir, I really need to go now. My colleague is waiting."

He shook his head, eased himself from the desk, and hooked his hand round her waist. "Dinner is what I ask for. You will not realize I am the best thing that would happen to you."

Her face turned red. "Excuse me, sir?"

"Oh, I am sorry." He reluctantly pulled his hand away. "I didn't know this will offend you."

"Of course, it offends me."

She was about to walk out of his office when he spoke.

"When was the last time you had fun with a man, Grace?" he asked coyly.

"Sir?" Her nostrils flared.

"Never mind." He walked to his desk. "I have this feeling we are going to be seeing more of each other. If you understand what I mean." He winked.

She managed a smile. "I really have to be going, sir."

Without waiting for his permission, she hurried out of the office.

The sun sucked on her skin as she walked out of the magnificent tall building, a reminder of how hot a typical sunny day could be in Lagos.

"I was wondering what was keeping you, Ma." Chuka gave her a knowing look.

Grace ignored him and entered into the Toyota Corolla that served as the company car. She hated the helpless feeling she was having at the moment. If not that she had to do her job and get the contract signed to their advantage, she would have given Mr Cookey a piece of her mind.

"What a jerk," she muttered.

"Ma?" Chuka responded.

She dismissed him with a wave of her hand.

They were already on their way back to the office when she remembered that she needed to be in church to see the pastor's wife—she had promised her mother.

"Whatever that made you and Ken divorce can be sorted out. Do not make the mistake I made. I lost a good man because of my pride," her mother had said the last time she'd visited.

What was Grace going to be discussing with the pastor's wife? Not that she had been to church after the pastor had preached on divorce and consequences. She was his topic—an example of what would happen to women who would want to leave their marriages.

She felt the vibration of her phone and picked it up.

'Hi, just checking on you, hope you are ok. Mr Adekola is inviting both of us to his wife's birthday next weekend at his place, and he doesn't know we are no longer together. Can you come? Let me know, please. Ken'

She stared at the message.

'... Just checking on you ...' He was deliberately ignoring last Saturday. Same way he had ignored the divorce as if it had never happened. She knew he was hurting, yet, he had gone around like his life was fine while she had died a thousand times.

CHAPTER SEVEN

Imelda pulled herself into a sitting position, examined the marks on her body, and swallowed a sob. She had gotten used to being beating by her man, as he had always come home to apologize. However, he hadn't apologized today.

"You make me crazy … always trying to control me." He had blamed her and had left the house.

She felt her heart tighten, the throbbing in her head, reminding her how long she had sat like a frightened child on the bed. Tears stung her eyes as if she had sand in them. She swung her legs, brought them to the cold floor, swayed out of the room, and managed to get outside.

"Imelda, you dey okay?" Mama Ruky, her neighbour, asked.

"Hmm," she replied with a nod while avoiding Mama Ruky's eyes.

She winced as she hunched to pick her slippers, dusted the doormat, walked back inside, and shut the door before Mama Ruky could start with her sermon of "kick a man who has turned into a parasite out of your life." She knew she was referring to Ahmad and had warned her to stay off her relationship. After all, her husband had been sleeping with Kudirat, her maid.

She went to the kitchen cabinet, took out a card of Panadol, threw two tablets inside her mouth, and pushed it down her throat with water. She took the glass back to the sitting room, sipped, and dropped it on the table close to her.

The first time Ahmad beat her, he had accused her of mocking him with poverty. What was her crime? Two pieces of meat in the soup she'd brought to him for dinner.

"How can you give me just two slices of meat... Have you reduced me to this level?" he had bellowed, telling her she reminded him of his joblessness. Then came the slap, the kicks, the choking.

One hitting done mistakenly gave birth to another, then another, and yet another, until it became part of their relationship, the marks on her body becoming a symbol of their union.

She wiped her nose, groped over the worn-out leather sofa for her phone which was ringing for the second time.

"Hello," she said.

"Hi, it's me, Kolawole."

She didn't remember any Kolawole.

"The guy that gave you a lift two days ago ..."

"Oh. I remember now." The angel that was there at the right time to save her from more shame. She recalled the smile he had given her when she had tried to cover her naked breasts from him. His scent when he had offered his jacket to her. Yes, she remembered him, all right.

"I just want to know that you are fine," he said.

"Yes, I am. Thank you so much, thank you for your help."

That was the only thing he had asked of her, her number, and she had given it to him.

"You sound tired. Please have some rest," he said.

"Okay. Thank you once again," she replied.

"Can I call you tomorrow?"

"Ehm ... No. Please, I will be fine."

That night, Ahmad did not return. She lay alone, and her sleep was everything but peaceful.

CHAPTER EIGHT

"Girlfriend, that girl has been screwing the boss right under our noses, and we didn't know?" Mary said.

Grace wondered how Mary would react if she knew that she, Grace, had known for a while and had even seen both of them making out in the office.

"How do you know this, Mary?" she asked, feigning ignorance.

"I ran into her three days ago being disgraced by no other but Mrs Ogungbeso," Mary said, rolling her eyes and ducking her head.

"Really! That's serious o, was it so bad?" Grace asked, genuinely concerned this time.

"You said bad? Girlfriend ... she was disgraced down to her undies. Boss Madam tore her into shreds." Mary was excited.

"Oga o, I pity the poor girl," Grace said.

"Wait, babe, you pity who? Don't tell me you are feeling for a girl that snatched another woman's husband," Mary interjected.

"No, but to strip a lady on the street because you suspect she is sleeping with your husband is just not cool at all."

"Babe, Imelda deserves what she got! She is reaping where she did not sow. Boss Madam is only protecting her territory."

"Mary, I'm not supporting what Imelda is doing with the boss, but let's look at it this way. Isn't it better for Madam to face her husband at home and deal with him in any way she deems fit, instead of facing the lady?"

"What if it was Imelda who seduced the man?" Mary countered.

"And what if it was the boss who lured her into it? Probably threatened her job or something," Grace reasoned.

"I don't know, but … I know that no lady will try that with my husband o. I will kill somebody the day I notice anything as little as a suspicious text message," Mary assured herself and her friend.

"You will not do anything, Mary … no be you again? You will only cry your eyes out and then resign to your fate, like a typical Nigerian wife," Grace joked.

"No o, ha Grace is like you don't know me o, I will not leave, for what now? For another woman like little Imelda to come and eat of my labour? God forbid, I will scatter … I will make life miserable for my husband and the woman."

"Ah, ah, Mary! Calm down na, na joke o, e never reach quarrel. Beside Oga Mike is not going to cheat on you anytime soon, or is he?" Grace was laughing now.

"No now, my Mike will not try such rubbish with me, he loves me too much to try that," Mary answered.

Imelda walked into Grace's office with a tray and a cup of tea.

"I did not see you when I came in this morning, Imelda." Grace took the cup of tea and sipped from it.

"I was here earlier, ma'am, but the boss called me to make his coffee," Imelda answered.

"Hmm ..." Mary snorted.

"And what happened to the boss's PA, Mrs Martins?" Grace asked her, ignoring Mary.

"Ehm … she … she … The boss said Mrs Martins is very busy and he wanted me to bring his coffee to him."

"Some people would not learn to leave other people's husbands alone until they are bathed with acid ..." Mary cut in.

"Mary!" Grace warned her friend.

"What!" Mary rolled her eyes. "Anyway—" she stood up and made for the door. "—I'm going back to my office. Call me for lunch."

She looked at Imelda sternly and walked out.

"Go back to your desk, Imelda. Check my appointments and get back to me. Send that email to Wilson group, and write the proposal for Unique Homes advert contract."

"Okay, ma'am."

"And Imelda?"

"Yes, ma'am?"

"See me before the end of the day. I need to talk to you."

The dark stripes on Imelda's legs had caught her attention for the second time that week, and she had wanted to ask her about it earlier. The young woman had been keeping to herself lately, not that she was a chatterbox like Mary. Still, being her personal assistant of six years, Grace knew she had lost her glow.

*

Four days to the party, and she had not given a reply yet. Not even an acknowledgement.

You are trying to saddle a dead horse. Was he pushing too hard? He should have accepted it was over when she did.

You are my wife, Grace. You will come back to me.

That was four years ago, and he wasn't sure if waiting was worth it.

He hadn't wanted to give her a divorce, but her lawyer had insisted. "You have to understand, Mr

Kenneth, that it is not up to you now. She wants her freedom."

Didn't they say that if you love someone, you have to let them go? Love can make one do stupid things.

First, he had blamed himself for making her do what she did. I should have listened more to her. But he realized it wasn't utterly his fault. She had married him on her terms, just as she was doing now—coming and going on her conditions.

"Oga, the truck driver said him no go collect eight thousand Naira for the supply o," one of his workers reported to him.

"How much him wan collect?" Ken asked.

"Oga him say na twelve thousand o."

"He is a thief! Tell him that I said so. Is he carrying Zuma Rock? Abeg find another truck for me," he angrily ordered.

He had not called Grace after the night they'd had dinner in his house when he'd revisited the incident that had led to their divorce. He knew she had cried. He blamed himself for making her cry, but he was hurting, too, not being able to talk about it with anyone these past years.

"I don't believe you, Kenneth. I know how you adore that woman and how she also adores you. Please don't give me this your incompatibility lies, I'm not a kid," his mother had said, wanting to know what had happened between them.

"Mama, I am not lying. We just realized that I cannot keep up with her demanding job," he had insisted.

"Did she catch you with another woman?"

"No, Mama! Haba! What makes you think that I will cheat on my wife?"

"Are you not the person that told me now that you cannot keep up with her demanding job?"

He had lied to get her back to him. He could just as well go to the party alone, but he wanted to see her. He hated to admit it, but he'd realized he still loved that woman. He'd never stopped loving her.

The bleeping of his phone jerked him up. He grabbed it, suddenly feeling energized as he saw her name.

'I'm thinking about it, will give you an answer by tomorrow. How are you, Kay?'

"Fair enough," he said with relief.

CHAPTER NINE

"Hello, who is this?"

With the phone held firmly to her ear with her shoulder, Grace typed rapidly on her laptop. She had ignored the call earlier. However, she wouldn't be able to finish her work with an annoying, persisting phone buzz. She waited impatiently for the caller who seemed not to be in a hurry.

"Finally, she decided to speak to me," said the excited voice at the other end.

She rolled her eyes and shook her head. "Who am I on with, please?"

With her eyes on the screen, she picked the cup of tea on the small table beside her and took a sip.

"Can you guess?" the caller said coyly.

"Look, I can't do this right now. It's either you tell me who you are or get off. I am very busy right now."

"Wow, lady! You work at home, too? Now you fascinate me ..."

She yawned. The leather sofa squeaked as she shifted her butt and rested her head. "I don't think I want to continue this conversation really."

"Okay, it's me, Morgan."

"Which Morgan?" she asked.

"Oh, girl, you break my heart. Have you forgotten so soon?"

Grace made an abrupt stop.

"What?" she shouted.

"Surprise, I guess." The caller laughed softly.

"How did you get my number?" she asked with clenched teeth.

"Money talks, babe. Money talks." He laughed again.

"It's not funny, Mr Cookey. I want to know who gave you my private number," she insisted.

"I can get anything I set my heart on, including your number, babe."

"You have my office number."

"I need to call you anytime, day or night. Don't forget, you still work for me," he answered.

"I don't think you got my number just for the sake of the job we are doing for your company," she accused.

"Ehm ... no ..."

"So what do you want?" She folded one of her legs.

"What do you think I want?" he teased.

"I don't know."

She wriggled her nose as the scent of a burn filtered into the sitting room where she was. She sprang up and scurried into the kitchen, put the pot down, flapped her fingers, and grimaced out of pain.

"And there goes my dinner," she muttered, the phone still to her ear.

"Let me treat you to a nice dinner," came the voice from the other end.

Not bad—she actually needed the conversation, someone to pull her away from her addiction to work.

"I know a nice place."

"You are joking, seriously," she said and walked back to the sitting room. "What do you want, Mr Cookey?"

"I want you. And I never joke with anything I want, so I am asking again. Grace, please date me."

"I can't believe you, sir. You don't even know me. We only met last week. How can—"

"It takes just a day to know someone, and knowing a formidable lady like you will be a nice job I want to take up," he cut in.

"You know what, sir?"

"Call me Morgan."

"Morgan ... I can't date you. Please accept that." She smiled. She would pay anything to see his sunken face right now. Proud man that thinks the sun rose and set when he said so.

He was silent for a while. "I will not force you into doing anything, Grace, but I will like you to promise me you will think about this."

There was really nothing to think about as far as she was concerned, but she wanted to get him off her back and her phone.

"Are you?" he continued.

"Am I what? Oh! Sure, I will think about it."

"Okay, that's better. Thank you."

Good. Let him chew on that, but based even on the little time she had been with him, she knew a man like Morgan Cookey would not want to back down so soon.

"You and I are the same—you are good at what you do, I don't play with my business, we can make a good team, and I am not playing. I can make you part of my company as long as you would be by my side."

A ridiculous offer he had made to her earlier that day.

Grace leaned forward and hunched towards her laptop, punched some keys, and her mind wandered again. Morgan would have been the kind of man she could consider—he owned and ran not just a company, but a conglomerate. He would understand when a woman wanted to build a career for herself.

Her phone beeped, and she grabbed for it. A glance at the message that came in and every thought of a dinner date with another man felt like a sin.

'Thank you so much, Sweet, I am expecting a positive response, sorry for the last time, I have missed you so much. Kay'

CHAPTER TEN

"Oga Ken, good evening, sir."

Chinyeaka angled her body towards the man that occupied her mind. Each time she planned to approach him, make him see her, he would walk past without a glance. His aloofness did nothing to ease her desire, though.

"Ehen ... How are you doing?" Ken answered, washed food particles off his hands, and stood with his friend, about to leave the restaurant.

"I'm very fine, sir," she replied, smoothing her weave-on.

She had never had to beg for attention from men. This one was different. The first time she'd set her eyes on him was the day she had decided he would be hers. Everything about him was breath-taking.

"Chinyeaka, didn't you also see me here?" Edu rebuked her angrily.

"Sorry, sir, I didn't see you," she pleaded. "Oga Ken, can you please buy lunch for me?"

She'd said the only thing that came to mind. Oh, how she wanted to disappear—he would think she was a hungry, beggarly lady. Wasn't she? A salesgirl at Odu-Ade market ... The life of a salesgirl was similar to that of a pauper, but not this sales girl. Not her.

He stared at her with a toothpick stuck between his teeth. Those eyes—he had given her the pleasure of looking at them. Her knees went weak, and she felt flushed. I love him already.

"Here." He handed a five hundred naira note. "This should do," he said and walked out with Edu.

*

It was past eight-thirty by the time Chinyeaka got to her house at Moshalashi Street. She wrinkled her nose as she parted the torn curtain that demarcated the room from the space they now used as a kitchen. She hated the place; it smelt of poverty and hopelessness.

"You are late today," her cousin said.

She hated it whenever she did that—making her feel like she was a little girl and her cousin was her mother.

"I went to church."

She didn't care if her cousin bought that; she was dumb, after all. She picked a plastic cup, sniffed it before fetching water from a gallon. This is not the life; she had promised herself she would not end up like some of her mates in the village nor her cousin whose salon shop was on the verge of closing.

"A friend invited me." She dropped the cup, gawped at the pot of soup her cousin was stirring, and her lips curled up. Who makes this kind of soup now in Lagos?

"And when did you start attending church programs?" Her cousin shot her a glance. "I know you very well, Chinyeaka. You would not lose your Telemundo series 'King of hearts' to attend to any church program. Besides, you have not even been to any church for the past month."

She regarded her cousin for a while and looked away. "As I have a lot of negative things happening in my life, I have to follow my friend to the deliverance program in their church."

"Did he pray for you?" her cousin asked curiously.

"Yes, now."

She went back into the room, sprawled on the only mattress in the stuffy space. Wriggling her nose again, she couldn't stand the disgusting odour from the public toilet at the back of the house which had infiltrated the whole house.

"Thank God for you o." Her cousin joined her later.

"Hallelujah!" she muttered.

Chinyeaka never knew she was this good at lies and fabricating stories. She had followed Ken to church, had carefully scanned through the pews and spotted him at the third row, located his car in the parking lot, and had hung around it.

"Oga Ken, good evening, sir," she had greeted.

"Oh! Nne, do you attend this church? I have not seen you here before," he had asked.

"Yes, sir. I always sit at the back, sir," she'd lied so smoothly.

He had offered her a lift. "Which side are you going, so I can drop you?"

This had made her smile to herself—all she had wanted would soon be hers. "I no dey go far sir, just the other road."

While her heart sang, she needed to be seen as desperate.

"No worry, it's already late. Let me drop you."

The interior of his Toyota Avalon 2015 model had blown her away. The cold air from the A/C had hit her in the face and sent a cold chill through her body down to her toes as she sank into the soft car seat. She'd blessed the woman who had left Oga Ken for girls like her.

The incredible voice of Rihanna on 'We Found Love' saturated every part of the car as they drove in silence. She sang along, moving her body and brushing against his arm, his hand on the gear.

When he dropped her at the junction that led to her street, she wished he would have stayed a little longer to watch her swing her hips for him as she walked home, but he'd zoomed off immediately as her legs had touched the ground.

"Do you want food?" her cousin asked.

"No! They gave us food there."

She would leave this place without turning back, become somebody's wife—definitely Oga Ken. She liked him, and it wouldn't be long until he would start feeling the same way. She would make sure of that.

She sat on her side of the bed, couldn't sleep. She envied her cousin, who was fast asleep after the heavy Eba and egusi soup. She kept reminiscing on the beautiful moments in his car, the scent of his cologne, the feel of his hand on her bare arm as he'd helped her with the seatbelt. She'd wanted his hand to linger, but it had been over before she knew it.

She needed to get closer to him, so he could see her not like any other sales girl but as a woman capable of satisfying him and filling his loneliness. She must come up with a plan.

The thought lingered in her mind and sent her to sleep finally.

*

That same night, Grace woke up to a tap at her door. She was afraid to open at first, but when she peered through the door hole, Imelda was there, in her nightgown, hair unkempt, eyes swollen and red, bruises on her lips.

Grace quickly opened the door, pulled her into an embrace, and allowed her to cry on her shoulder.

She'd had a long talk with the younger woman in the office earlier.

"Here, find your way to my house if you are in trouble," she had said.

She didn't understand why a woman as beautiful as Imelda would hang on to a violent man. A cheating man, she would understand—ladies no longer walked away from cheating partners nowadays. "It rains everywhere," they would say. Not that she saw herself enduring a cheating man.

But a violent man? That was crazy. In fact, she'd gone mad when Imelda had told her how long it had been going on and that the idiot was the reason she had to sleep with the boss—to get him a freaking job!

"Come here, dear." She patted the other woman on the back. "Let it all out."

He had beaten her again, dragged her out of the house in her nightgown, and shut the door.

Imelda refused to eat; she stared into nothing like a deranged woman. Grace took her to her room, cleaned her bruises, covered her with the only duvet in there, and went back to the sitting room where she slept until morning.

CHAPTER ELEVEN

"Hei! Didn't you see me? Abi I don small for your eye? Girlfriend … tell me what occupies your mind this morning?" Mary asked.

Before Grace could utter a word, Mary squealed, jumped, and clapped with a gleam in her eyes. "I totally forgot!"

She took Grace by the hand and pulled her towards her office.

"What is it now, Mary? Did you win a lottery?" Grace said, running after her, amused.

"Better than that, girlfriend." She pushed Grace inside the office and closed the door behind them. "Taraaaa!"

She gestured at the bunch of white flowers, two boxes of chocolates, and a note on the desk.

Grace picked the little card inside one of the boxes of chocolates and read:

'You have occupied my mind from the first day I met you. Please go on a date with me tonight, Grace. From a lovesick man.'

"This doesn't sound like Ken," she muttered.

She had spoken with him last night—a cordial and beautiful conversation, one of the very few good discussions they had had after their divorce. She had told him about Imelda, and he'd given sensible advice. They had finally settled with her agreeing to come to the birthday party with him on Saturday.

He would be picking her up at noon. He was so happy that she could hear that baby-like laugh of his. The laughter that came out whenever he either heard good news, had eaten a delicious meal, or wanted to seduce her into having sex with him.

Maybe this was his way of expressing his joy, but … Ken has never been a flower or chocolate lover, she thought as she checked out the arrangement and boxes of chocolates.

"Of course, it can't be from Ken. Has he finished counting his containers and his monies? He is not this romantic abeg," Mary said with a hiss.

"Eh-eh! Please stop it, don't insult him, please. He may not be as romantic as you described, but he was enough for me," Grace defended.

"Hmm, yet you left him," Mary said, making a face.

"I didn't leave him because of that. He was romantic enough for me while we lasted. It wasn't his fault that we divorced."

"Ehm … I'm sorry for bringing this up, but all these did not come from him," Mary said.

"It's okay. So who brought them?" Grace asked.

"Oh! I don't know o o, it was brought here by a delivery man. You were not around, so I received them," Mary said with a mouth full of chocolate.

"You don't know, and you are already eating? Mary, one day, you will die of longer throat o," Grace joked.

"How that one take concern me? My own is to chop. Your headache is to figure out where they came from," Mary said, stretching her hands to collect another chocolate.

Grace snatched the box from her, took the flowers, and hurriedly left for her own office.

"See, don't finish the chocolate o, you will have a runny stomach," Mary shouted. "And don't forget to gist me on who our romantic dude is."

"Mary, mind your business!" she responded as she walked down the hall.

She had barely taken her seat when she got his message.

'Was I able to convince you into going out with me tonight? I really miss you and would want to hear from you again, my elegant woman.'

She dialled his number.

"Hey."

"Hey," he replied.

"You really shouldn't have gotten me all these. I won't change anything about what I told you the last time." Her polished nails drummed on the desk.

"I am not asking for too much, Grace," he replied.

"I told you that I will not date you, not now, not tomorrow, not ever. Please just find another woman who would appreciate you."

Maybe she should give him a try, who knows. He may be what she needed to get Ken off her mind.

"Why?" he asked.

She did not answer immediately.

Ken, that was why—what would he say? How would he look at her? She bit her lip. She wanted to flush him out of her system, and this would be the opportunity.

Then there was the problem of what people would think of her. She'd just got divorced and was ready to jump into another relationship in four years? Though four years was okay to move on, people might not see it that way.

She shook her head. She had moved on now, and Ken should, too, maybe. He may also be hanging out with another woman.

"Are you still there?" he asked from the other side of the line.

"Ye ... yes ..." She cleared her throat.

"Is it because of your ex-husband?"

The question hit her right in the head. Even though she wouldn't admit it, deep down, she had wanted Ken to come back, to forgive her and love her again. She wished it was Ken that had brought the flowers and chocolates, asking her out for a date. Not Morgan.

She was also afraid her first marriage had been a mistake that would have been avoided assuming they'd realized their differences before allowing passion and lust to make decisions for them. She would never be the woman Ken wanted and didn't trust herself to be a devoted mother to any child, which was what he wanted.

"Please don't ... don't ask me that. I just want to be alone to sort myself out, that is all," she said.

"Okay, I don't have any problem with that, but at least go on a friendly date with me tonight. I will not pressure you into reciprocating my attraction to you if you don't want to," Morgan said after a long pause.

"Just a date?" she asked.

"Just a date" he assured.

"Okay, I will try."

"I will gladly pick you anywhere you want me to."

"Just give me the venue, and I will find my way, that is if I don't change my mind later."

"Don't break a man's heart by saying 'no'," he joked.

"That's emotional blackmail, and it's not fair." She managed a smile.

CHAPTER TWELVE

A mad fat woman fighting with almost everyone in the bus, a crazier bus conductor, a preacher whose coat reminded her of the one her father had that later turned into an abode for roaches, not to mention a seat neighbour whose mouth smelled like a gutter—she regretted refusing Mary's offer to give her a ride home. To Hell with the pepper soup! She could have as well prepared any other thing for herself and Imelda that would not involve going to the market.

She had called Morgan to tell him she would not meet up for the dinner date. Though disappointed, he had understood but insisted she should call him if she changed her mind.

In a short while, voices with different keys rose in the cacophony. Grace wasn't one to join in religious rituals in buses or public places. She remembered Ken would always tell her that if not for him, she would have been an atheist, whenever they had arguments about religion.

By the time she finally got home, Imelda was gone. The leather chair creaked as she collapsed in it and kicked her shoes off. Somehow, she'd known this would happen. She tried her number again, but it was still switched off, so she dropped a message. "How are you doing, Imelda? Got home and didn't see you. Give me a call as soon as you can."

She prowled the house—no particular thing in mind to do. She picked her phone to call Ken and decided against it. It was one thing to admit how she craved him. To confess this to him would be a disaster, and that's what she would be doing if she kept calling.

She exhaled deeply and called Morgan, took a quick shower, applied a little lipstick, and walked out with her purse.

*

Grace walked into the NOK restaurant on Victoria Island, Lagos. Fondling her purse, she combed the seats for him, her gaze finally resting on him already approaching her. Her Kali ankle strap shoes clicked on the marble floor as she walked to him, and they met mid-way.

"You finally made it," Morgan said with a smile.

She pulled away as he brought his lips close to her face, offering her hand instead.

"I didn't know what to do with myself," she said and followed him to a table.

"Wine first …" He thrust his chest out. "I don't know what you like so … I have to wait." His eyes smouldered. "Forgive me, lady … You are beautiful tonight."

She cleared her throat, shot him a quick glance.

"Thank you. I am ready to make a choice." His brows arched. "On the wine," she emphasized.

She wished she could feel something for him. He seemed like a nice guy, with a little pinch of pride, though, but which rich man didn't have that?

"Oh, wine … yes … sure." He pulled his gaze from her. "I thought you were speaking about something else."

He narrowed his eyes with a smirk on his face.

A flirty one. She would have laughed out loud. Anyway, he was doing an excellent job with his flirting technique—just, it wasn't getting to her. Okay, she needed to enjoy the moment with him. Something may change between them.

They finally settled for a white, Zinfandel. Her first time, so she didn't know what to expect when she lifted the wine glass to her lips.

"You look distracted, Grace," Morgan said, observing her from the corner of his eye.

"I have not been here before," she replied, looking towards the live band.

"Sincerity! I like that about you. You don't pretend."

She gave a weak smile and sipped some more wine. She had thought this would be fun. "Let your hair down!" everyone had told her, but it wasn't working. Her mind wasn't ready for this, yet she wished it was.

He took her hand from across the table, gently stroking. "Grace, there is something else bothering you. What is it? Who is taking your attention away from me?"

She looked in the other direction from him, her cheeks burning with shame. He was right—her attention was somewhere else, stolen by someone she'd left years ago.

"Excuse me." She pushed her chair backwards as she stood. "I have to use the ladies'."

She left in a hurry, not even knowing where the ladies' was.

"Ken, why are you doing this?" she muttered under her breath.

When she finally found it, she strode in, shut the door, and collapsed against it. She was a mature woman capable of making decisions to suit her. Why did it feel like she was cheating on Ken? And for Christ's sake—she shouldn't be thinking of him and having warm thoughts in the presence of another man!

She hunched over the washbasin and gazed at her reflection in the mirror. She had to get a grip and enjoy the dinner.

She managed a better composure when she came out, flashing Morgan a smile while she took her seat. "I am so sorry about that, have a lot on my mind."

"I am sure you do … but you are here now." He leaned forward and poured her more wine. "With me, I want all of you tonight, babe."

She couldn't help but laugh. Not bad, after all.

"You know my PA I told you about?" She sipped from her glass.

"Mmhmm …" Morgan affirmed while swallowing some more wine.

"I came back, and she was nowhere to be found, probably has gone back to that … that bastard," she added under her breath.

If Morgan was surprised, he didn't show it.

"Oh," was all he said.

"I don't know how I feel about this. I am sad, disappointed, you know?" she continued.

"Hold on, Grace. These things happen, an abused woman going back to her abuser. It's not new, and besides, we are here to enjoy the evening, not to brood over some stupid girl that doesn't know what she wants."

"Oh, right." She wanted to talk, not bore him to death with silence, but it seemed she'd chosen the wrong topic.

Ken would have listened to every word she said; he would have allowed her to "brood over some stupid girl who doesn't know what she wants."

"It's like you are a regular here." She desperately needed something to discuss.

"Why do you ask?"

"The way you fit in immediately. The bartenders and the waiters already know your name. Even that singer acknowledged you with a nod," she pointed out.

His face was upturned. At least she was able to make him smile; one good score. She was beginning to think the whole thing would turn into a solemn assembly. He was a handsome man, she observed secretly, with a well-structured jaw, well-trimmed white and black beard, almost flawless skin that looked like a ceramic floor. Not so chiselled and no vein snaking under his skin; he would have made the right partner if only she could get her emotions up for him.

"... So it seems you have not been to many intercontinental restaurants yourself."

Grace only heard this part of all he had been saying. He must have been recounting many of such top restaurants he had been to worldwide.

"Not quite so many," she said, not wanting to sound too local. "I personally have a thing for our local dishes, so I prefer to go to restaurants that can prepare our local delicacies without adding any Oyibo spice."

They both laughed at this.

"I hope you will enjoy this place. I actually chose here to give you a special treat."

She sensed his pride and felt pity for him. If only he knew ...

"Sure, the place is beautiful. The serenity, the music, the setting, the waiters. I feel like a queen already," she said genuinely.

"So, why don't you want to be my lady?" Morgan asked with food in his mouth.

"I thought we would not go into this discussion. You promised this would be just a dinner date," she said politely.

"I know I said that, but can't you see? I like you. You are elegant, poised, beautiful, and intelligent. We are good together. We can build empires. We will go places. Please, Grace, don't turn me down," he pleaded.

"Morgan, you a good man with a good heart. You are handsome, wealthy, full of life, and fun to be with, but … Believe me when I say I can't. I need some time to make this decision. Give me time. I don't want to be under pressure."

They said little to each other while they ate, but she caught him staring several times, the longing evident on his face.

"Thank you for tonight," she muttered and fled before he could say a word.

It was a mess really, going to a date with Ken tagging along in her mind.

"Wait!" Morgan scuttled to where she stood, turned her to face him. "Am I that bad?"

She shook her head violently, fighting the tears that had welled up in her eyes. She hated how she couldn't be with another man without Ken intruding; he was always there in her mind.

He is not as light-hearted as Ken … His eyes don't excite me like Ken's … Ken would have said this instead of that …

"You were not with me throughout the night," he continued. "Maybe I should step up my wooing game." He chuckled.

She blinked away a few tears and shook her head. "No, it was me …"

Another chance of getting herself a relationship blown away. She wasn't looking for a serious commitment, and Morgan was that kind of man who would understand. "I know your kind, not meant to be caged," he had said earlier.

"I have to go now," she mumbled and disengaged from his hold, then walked briskly towards her apartment.

"Let me give you a ride back," he offered.

She accepted. The ride was silent, and she alit the second he stopped. Still, he followed her, touched her shoulder to stop her.

"Morgan, I have to go."

Thankfully, he nodded and went back into his car, drove off. She turned towards her house and stopped mid-stride, gaze fixed on a silhouette against her fence. The figure eased himself off the wall and approached.

"Ken."

Her breath caught in her throat. His face looked clouded, the fire in his eyes speaking volumes.

He masked his ashen face with a smile, except for the sadness in his eye.

"Had a good night?" He stood away from her. She felt a stab of shame. "If you had told me … I wouldn't have come."

Her gaze followed him as he walked towards his car.

"I … didn't, er … plan for it … it was just—" She shook her head. "Nothing … It was nothing." Her legs followed. "You didn't tell me you would come."

If she were a child, she would have thrown herself on the ground and wailed. Maybe it would have made him turn back.

"The Chinese company I trade with has decided to make me one of their permanent partners. I wanted to celebrate with you." He shrugged. "Bad timing, I guess." A nervous laugh followed.

Mouth open, she swallowed. The day hadn't turned as perfect as she wanted. Why did she even agree to go on a date?

"We can still celebrate." She didn't want him to leave her alone.

He turned and stared at her intently, then erased the distance between them. She felt his warm breath on her face. Oh, God! The intoxicating scent … She licked her lips and lowered her gaze.

"Did he kiss you?" His eyes flared.

"What?" She searched his face.

"It's late, Grace. Go in now …" He walked to his car and drove off.

She covered her mouth with her hands, yet her pain couldn't be suppressed. Nor her longing.

*

Ken drove at a low speed, not in a hurry to get home.

I was a fool to have thought she would be here for me.

He laughed softly at himself.

He had been eager to break the news to her, knowing both of them had worked, prayed, and wished for this day. She was the one who wrote the proposals; she had sent mails to 'Livi-Virony Ceramic Company.' He was invited to meet with the board of directors, and the meeting led to him looking for a big and suitable area to site the company. Another one from Grace—she wrote to the state government, wrote to their bank. And after securing the land, nothing was heard from the Chinese company until last week, when he got a call of their planned visit to Nigeria and that they would want to see him.

It was one of the proudest moments of his life. All the while he was there, he'd thought of her as the energy behind this success. He'd wished she was by his side, had imagined her excitement.

All those sweet memories had vanished like a fog when he'd seen her coming down from a stranger's car. Jealousy had tightened his heart. She was so beautiful—with another man! How could she do this? She'd moved on so easily without giving him a second thought.

His thoughts darkened.

He couldn't get over the divorce—no, over her. He was madly in love with Grace like he had never loved before. That's why it hurt so much. She had him locked up in her heart. Sometimes, he got angry thinking about her and wished her gone for good. Other times, he hoped she would come running back.

She is with another man.

What had he been thinking? That she would remain unmarried or no other man would approach her? His thoughts turned, despite himself, to the other man. He hadn't seen him clearly, but he'd seen how he had scurried to her side, touching her everywhere. Ken hissed.

This new man … Did she love him? Had they had sex?

What does it matter?

He hadn't believed she had moved on until today.

*

"Give us another chance, please!"

Heartless—that was what he had called her.

"You ran off because you wanted me to die, you know I can't live without you." A night without her, and he had threatened to kill himself. "You will forever live with the guilt when I am gone."

It wasn't the first time he had threatened her with his death, but Imelda was afraid he would carry out his threat one day when he got too lonely.

"It was a mistake … I was angry … Please come back." He was persistent, calling and texting, begging for her attention.

She had come back to him to prove her loyalty. She sniffed. Wasn't that what love was about? He needed her, and she couldn't stay away—one night was already too long. She couldn't stand him being helpless.

She was right; Ahmad was already wasted when she got home, had taken a higher dose of coke, sprawled naked on the floor, clothes, empty spirit bottles, half-eaten plate of rice littering the small sitting room, and very close to him was a tiny box containing a small amount of cocaine.

She had dragged him like a dead weight to the bed and left him still uncovered. Hands on her waist, she had taken in the whole scene. He had promised not to do drugs again. "Since you don't like it." But she had allowed him cigarettes.

Sex. That was what he compensated her with—or rather, she paid for neglecting him and making him go back to drugs. Hard sex, one of the ways he spoke to her, pouring his anguish with his cum. It was one of the reasons she was still hanging with him, sex. Just that she didn't like it with him anymore.

As she browsed through her call history, she noticed a familiar number and dialled.

"Hi," she breathed the word.

"Hi, it's Kola."

Her mouth curled up in a smile. His voice always soothed her in a fantastic way. Strange, she fluttered. Imelda didn't know if it was a good thing, though. She was afraid of falling for another man, but after visiting him at his workplace to hand over his coat, the way he had smiled shyly when he came out, an apron around his neck and patches of stains on him …

"I am a chef." He had grinned, his beard moving with his plump cheeks in a cute smile.

She'd known she may not be able to block him from her life. She saw what she had not seen in Ahmad: genuine kindness and simplicity.

"... The guy that gave you lift the other day."

She knew already—his voice gave him away.

"I have called before ..."

She turned to Ahmad who lay like dead meat on a butcher's table.

"... I was wondering if we could meet ..."

She would want to meet him, to look at his face and his small round lips that reminded her of a chubby baby.

"I don't know, Kola," she whispered, gave Ahmad a quick glance. "This is a bad time. Can I call you tomorrow morning?"

She ended the call without waiting for him to respond.

CHAPTER THIRTEEN

"You have been acting up since you came back from wherever it was you said you slept last night. You have been ignoring me, 'kilon shele, se'owa daada?' I am not understanding."

Neither was she. Watching him swallow balls of Eba covered with vegetable soup, Imelda wondered if he had relaxed and stopped seeking a job. How long would he comfortably rely on her to provide everything?

He stood up, dried his hands with a dirty cloth that hung on the connecting door between the room and the parlour, boxers pulled a little down to give his already protruding belly some comfort, exposing the line between his two butt cheeks and his pubic hair before his penis. She curled up her lips in disgust.

"Kosi'yonu' no problem, I am fine," she replied and moved forward to clear the table.

"Are you sure?" he asked, easing himself on a half-torn cushion and stretched lazily.

She nodded, bent to pick the plates and the bowl of dirty water. He slapped her butt, and she stiffened, trotted down to the kitchen, his laughter making her want to puke her guts out.

"Of course, you will be okay. After all, you are lucky to have someone like me, who knows how to make you happy. If I touch you now, you will begin to sing my name like a bird, Ahmad o ... do me like this o ... fuck me harder o ..." He laughed with pride. "Bring me water, abeg!" he shouted from the sitting room.

She could hear him smacking his lips from the kitchen. She brought the water and handed it over to him without a word. She detested the sound his throat made while he drank, the up and down movements of his Adam's apple.

Why hadn't she noticed the skin-recoiling mole at the corner of his mouth and the rashes on his neck? How long had these been there?

"Why are you looking at me like that?"

Startled, she took the cup and hurried back to the kitchen. The sudden disgust she felt surprised her. She was beginning to get mad at every little thing he did.

"Where you say you sleep last night, sef?" he asked behind her.

She continued washing the dishes, ignoring him.

"Where did you sleep last night?" he asked her again.

"I have told you I was at my Madam's house."

"And she allowed you to stay?"

She swallowed hard, trying to suppress the anger with the spittle that went down her throat. She squeezed her eyes tight, prayed he wouldn't utter another word.

"Simple play with you, to know if you would endure just a little, wait for me when things bad, you followed your 'ashawo' madam to her house," he continued.

His last sentence hit her like a bullet. How dare he call what he did to her 'play'? The bruises on her lips, the taste of her own blood on her tongue, the look on Mallam Isa's face when he came to urinate and saw her sitting outside, the many eyes looking at her from their windows like night owls, the mocking laughter from the landlord's wife when she was leaving the compound in the middle of the night ... and he called all that 'play'?

She folded her arms into a fist and took enough breath.

"Let me tell you, if you like be following useless women who have no man in their lives, you are the one that will regret it ..."

"Stop ... Ahmad, please stop," she murmured. She couldn't stand his words to her any more.

"What do you mean, 'Ahmad stop'? I am telling you the truth, Imelda. You are nothing without me. Forget this little job way you get, your life is empty without me, and you know it. How many men will look in your direction, you know now ... that is why you came back ... you have no option than to return. Forget that small drama way I act come dey beg you, I know you will come back ..."

She wanted so much to tell him that he lied—another man had not only picked interest in her but had asked her on a date! She would love so much to see the look on his face while he chewed on the revelation.

"Stop! Ahmad, stop!" she screamed.

He was taunting her, deliberately hurting her with words, daring her, drawing her into a battle she may likely not have the strength to fight. She had had enough and couldn't take any more.

"One more word ... just one more word ... and I promise you, you would not like the new colour of your skin by the time this hot water soaks your body," she said with clenched teeth.

Jaw dropped, and his head tilted backwards, he gazed at her for a while.

"You point a finger at me?" He coughed out a throaty laugh. "Imelda! You would bathe me with hot water? It's like you are mad!"

"I have done nothing but endure your lazy ass for the years we've been together ... I took in every rubbish you dished out every day because I thought you would be a better person ..." She trembled in anger. "And if you must know, things are going to change around here. If you think I will allow you the pleasure of kicking me around again? Then you don't know what is coming."

She shoved him aside with her shoulder and stomped out of the kitchen.

CHAPTER FOURTEEN

Ken neatly folded the architectural drawing and wiped beads of sweat that had formed on his forehead. Half of the day on the new site and it seemed they may not meet the deadline. The sun wasn't friendly, either, coming down as if it had a score to settle with the earth.

He was still contemplating going to grab a bottle of drink for the second time when he saw her. Jesus! Could it …

Hands crossed over his chest, his gaze swept over her, lingered on her hips. Trousers looked good on her, though she wore them not too often, except if she had changed her wardrobe. She was as beautiful as she had always been. The sun on her brown skin gave her a unique glow. Her red chiffon shirt, tucked inside her trousers, accentuated the shape of her breasts and her stomach—she had nothing except a black bra underneath.

He would have loved to give her nipples a pinch or two had they still been together. She may not like it now.

What was wrong with him? He was supposed to be angry after seeing her last night with another man. His heart rose as he took in air and exhaled. She was his little woman, always had been even when she walked away. He knew he had to get her back no matter what it would take.

His gaze followed her. Her smile became wider as she approached. As she cast her almond-shaped eyes on him, he couldn't help but smile back.

So much for feigning anger.

"You came?"

She nodded.

They both stood looking at each other, hearts swollen in pride. Yet, there was this painful reminder that it was no longer for both of them; they could no longer claim this glory together.

"It's nice here."

The hot air rattled the cellophane bag she held. With his eyes still on her face, he took a deep breath and nodded. "Hmm ..."

Without thinking, he gathered her in an embrace. She gasped, muscles tense. The pleasant scent from her hair filled his nostrils.

"New shampoo? I like it."

He felt her relaxing. She chuckled, and he tightened his arms around her. He missed her, the fire they ignited together, the passion—she was meant for him. Why didn't she see it?

"You did it," she said in his ear.

"No, we did it," he corrected and took possession of her lips.

He heard her moan and deepened the kiss. His tongue sought for the passion he knew was still there.

"Kay ..." she murmured, but he was too far gone with the ecstasy. He felt her soft hands on his chest as she gently pushed him away. "People are watching."

"Oh!" His head spun left, right, and left again before his gaze rested once more on her shy face. He hadn't planned to kiss her, but when her lustrous lashes had fluttered as she'd looked at him and her lips had slightly parted ... Well ...

"I am sorry, Grace." He cleared his throat.

"For what?' she asked, biting her lower lip.

"For kissing you." He wasn't actually sorry, though. He had wanted to do this long ago, to satisfy his curiosity that she still wanted him. A glint shone in her eyes. Her hunger wasn't hidden; she wanted him as much as he did her. That was a good sign. "I should have remembered you now belong to another man."

"Here, I got this for you." She handed the bag to him.

She deliberately avoided his last statement. He would not press her; seduction had always done it for him, though he doubted if that would work now.

He opened the bag, and his face widened with a childish grin. "Thank you, sweetheart."

At last, his hunger would be sated. He thanked her, and she nodded in response.

"Come, let me show you around. You will see some of the men working, too."

He asked how she got to know that he was there. She answered that she got to his office and found him absent. It was Edu, his friend, that told her where to find him.

Surprising that she would come looking for him, abandoning her work. Remorse? Was she here to explain last night? Hands in his pockets, shoulders raised high, he walked side by side with her.

"I just wanted to see you, at least to congratulate you properly," was her reply.

Ken pulled his hand from his pocket and took hers, stroking his fingers on hers. She didn't pull away. He had loved her from the day they'd met at the banking hall, when she had been screaming down the bank, demanding to see the manager. He had followed her out, requested her number and an opportunity to see her again. She had been reluctant at first, but he had persisted.

"I like you," he had told her.

She was petite, and he didn't observe how well-formed her hips were until they met again and she wore a short gown, like the one she'd worn to his house the other day.

"Kay?"

"Hmm?"

"About yesterday." She paused and lowered her gaze. "It was nothing really. I am so sorry."

He curled his hand around her small waist as they moved.

"I have never stopped seeing you as my wife, Grace, even when you made me sign those papers. I thought I had to set you free because I love you. I prayed you would look back and realize we could mend this …"

She said nothing.

"I don't want to move on, and later realized I didn't do all I could have done to keep you. I am a patient man, Grace. I will wait for you to sort yourself out but don't forget I am also a man, with blood running through my veins. I may not wait forever."

"Kay—"

"Come, let me see you to your car. Mr Lee is waiting for me," he cut in before she could say any other word. "Thank you for coming here, Grace. It really meant so much to me."

She nodded.

"Hope we are still meeting on Saturday?" His hands hung onto the door of her car.

"Hmm." She nodded in agreement, fumbled with her car keys before she turned on the ignition.

He watched her car disappear before walking back to the site. There was still something remaining. He had felt the spark just as he had the night she'd shown up drenched.

It gave him hope.

CHAPTER FIFTEEN

Imelda ambled towards her apartment. She was late again, and seriously, she didn't care. She had secretly wished Ahmad would question her about it. She halted as she met him outside the door, barricading the entrance with his body, smile plastered on his face.

"Ifemi, iyebiye mi, welcome back," he said and opened his arms for an embrace.

She tilted her head to the side and grimaced. Whenever Ahmad decided to be friendly, it would be because of two things—either he wanted to borrow money or sex. She narrowed her eyes at him.

"Are you not going to dismiss the person you were speaking to on the phone?"

Kolawole! She had gone on a dinner date with him, first time doing that with someone else beside Ahmad.

Kola had insisted on meeting after work, and had taken her to his house, treated her to a nice dinner. She didn't even remember what he'd called the dish he'd prepared. By God! She would eat anything he fed her, as long as he kept looking at her the way he had today. Watching him cook was a delight—whisking the eggs and flipping them in the pan. She had never imagined a man with an apron, but seeing it on Kola had made it beautiful.

"I am a chef," he had told her, observing her reaction.

Who cared if he was a security man? He was so gentle and fun to be with. "Do you mind if I … If you don't mind helping out … Please, can I …"

When was the last time a man had treated her with such respect? She knew he was avoiding asking her about the scenario that had brought them together, and she wasn't keen to discuss it.

"You have a man?"

He had done all the talking while she did all the laughing and nodding.

"So tell me, why did you decide to honour my invitation today, after rejecting my offers severally?" he had asked, but she hadn't heard him, had only seen his lips moving.

"Imelda, are you okay?" He'd looked at her, understood every face she made.

Why do the best things come when you are already stuck with the wrong one?

The food had been almost done, the sweet aroma filling the kitchen.

"Ye … yes … Sorry, I didn't get your question," she had confessed.

He'd looked at her with suspicion. She'd feared he'd already gotten a hint about her miserable life and was waiting for her to bring it up. He had repeated the question.

"Yes … Yes. I am okay."

She was, with him.

It was like every part of him reminded her of all that Ahmad was not and may never be.

He had been slowly wiping his hands with the kitchen towel and giving her furtive glances, eyes that made her knees tremble and her skin flush.

"Eh … Let me wait for you at the dining." She had eagerly escaped from embarrassing herself before him.

"The food is ready. You can help me set the table, that is, if you don't mind."

She hadn't known she was hungry until she tasted the delicacy, one of the best meals she had eaten in years after she'd left home. Both the food and the man that prepared it had soothed her spirit like the blue cloud over the mountain, and like spring water from a sacred fountain, it had lifted her.

'Thank you so much, Imelda. I am glad you gave me your time today," he had told her when he'd dropped her in front of the transformer before her street.

She had insisted he drop her there—she didn't want Ahmad to see her and get agitated like the last time. And he had called to make sure she had gotten home.

"Please let me call you back later, Kola," she said with her eyes still fixed on Ahmad.

Later that night, his hands crawled like the arms of an arachnid on her body. She recoiled and turned her back on him, shifting to the wall. He drew closer, planting kisses, running his tongue on her back, neck, her face. She knew what he wanted—sex, the only thing he was ever ready to do.

His touches became rough, like her mother's five-year-old dish sponge. His kisses suddenly grew heavy. His tongue made her cringe like the day a centipede had crawled on her bare thigh while she was sitting in their corridor.

"Sorry, Ahmad. I worked really hard, and I'm so tired," she lied.

"Come on, baby. I did everything for you today. A little appreciation would be nice," he complained.

That was it—Ahmad never did anything for free. Sex was the price for his earlier kindness.

"Ahmad, please, I'm sorry. I promise you that tomorrow will not be like this. I will give you what you want tomorrow ..."

"Oya just turn, let me just put it in and remove it," he pleaded.

She didn't respond to his plea, nor was she ready to allow him to take possession of her body, not that night. Meeting Kola had made her realize that she could be treated better and deserved much more than what she was getting.

*

Ken drove towards his gate.

As he tooted his horn, he caught sight of a figure crumpled in a sitting position by his gate, with a shawl around her neck. He couldn't recognize her at first, but as he got closer and she stood, her face became clearer.

"What are you doing here, Chinyeaka? It's late!" He pushed his head out from the window, and at the same time, the gate swung open. He drove in, and the girl followed.

"Oga, na your sister?" Baba, his gateman, asked.

"Baba, don't worry. Please lock the gate," he said while leading Chinyeaka inside the house.

"I have problems with my sister. She asked me to leave the house for her." She sobbed. "I don't know where to go to, sir ..."

"How did you find my place?" he asked, leaning against the wall and massaging his jaw. The girl sat opposite him, shoulders rocking with sobs.

"I know you stay here, sir ... I am sorry, sir. I didn't want to bother you. I only needed a place to stay for the night ..."

Strange. Surely, she could find a friend's house or even a colleague's place to go to, unless ...

"Everybody I know stays far from here. It wouldn't be easy to get to them this night." She stared at him with watery eyes. "This is the only place ..."

"Let me take you home to beg your sister." He eased his weight from the wall and walked towards her. "You cannot stay here."

"No, no, no … sir! Her boyfriend is with her. You don't want to go there." Her voice mellowed. "Trust me, sir."

He considered possible decisions.

"Okay … Let me get something for you to drink, then I can call your Madam and see if she could house you for the night," Ken said, dropping his keys on top of the designed wooden centre table.

He left her in the sitting room, went into the kitchen, and came out with a bottle of drink.

Words got stuck in his throat, and his jaw dropped, glued to the spot. Did he imagine it? Chinyeaka stood in his sitting room naked.

"I am offering you all this, sir. Let me show you what I can do," she said to him.

He shook his head, his nerves frozen with the chilled drink in his hand.

"What is this?" he asked coldly.

The girl got bolder. Her eyes fixed on his face, she walked towards him. "Abeg sir, I just want you to see me as a woman that can satisfy you. I will give you as many children as you want."

She was close. So close …

"Chinyeaka, please … Believe me … you don't want to do this." He stepped away from her.

"I want to do it, sir. I want you so much …"

She closed the gap. Shallow breath warmed his face.

"Chinyeaka! Chinyeaka, please … Put your clothes on and leave now. I understand how you feel, but I cannot give you what you want."

"Why, Oga Ken? Why can't you do it?"

He could easily hear the tremor in her voice.

Every second drew her more to where he stood. It was difficult not to notice her well-formed breasts, the way they bounced when she moved closer to him, the big black nipples looking at him, the lines that travelled down her womanhood. He wiped his wet palm on his shirt and turned towards the staircase.

"I have a woman who means a lot to me. Please close the door behind you when you are done wearing your clothes."

He was ascending the stairs when she spoke.

"Are you sure you are a man? Maybe you cannot get it up?"

He stopped. The turmoil in his mind turned to rage—he knew she was drawing her last straw.

"Get out of my house, young lady," was the last thing he said before he went into his room and locked the door.

*

What humiliation! She roughly wiped her face and continued walking. Blinded by tears, she stepped in a puddle, groaned as it splashed all over her legs. She had decided to go after a man and had met a brick wall. It had been the other way round since she was fifteen.

Chinyeaka wasn't that beautiful, but what she lacked on the face, she gained on her body. With hips like an earthen calabash and breasts like the traditional pots her grandmother used for water before she died, she was a stunner. She had to sieve through the many men who came after her.

At nineteen, she had fallen in love with a man from River State who had come to Calabar as a road worker and had moved in with him, an escape from the misery at home. He was her first—the one that unlocked her passion and exposed her to an insatiable lust for pleasure. She could have sworn he loved her until eight months later. He had left and hadn't come back, leaving her teenage heartbroken.

Then there was Jude and Udoh … Always moving in with them only to be conned later. She even had a child with one. Her young heart was still wobbling at the sight of men, trusting when she should have been discreet. She came to Lagos, got wiser—discarded love and decided to fuck around for the fun of it and of course, the money.

Ken was different. With him, she saw what she had not seen in those men—a rest from all her struggles. She wasn't asking for much but to be loved again. Now he'd rejected her, made her feel like an idiot.

"I have a woman I cherish."

An ex-wife who didn't consider him good enough. What a stupid man he was. When there was someone who would adore him … Why hang on to a smoke? She clutched her chest.

"I have a woman I cherish."

"Pwaa!" she spat. Like those other men—they always had another. Only that he had not fucked her. What difference did it make? More disgraceful, she must say, for he did not even find her attractive.

Whoever that woman was, she would find her.

CHAPTER SIXTEEN

What is he doing here?

"Grace! See who we have here, my favourite staff?" her boss hollered.

When big jobs and money are involved, everyone who can deliver becomes the favourite staff for him.

"Good morning, Mr Cookey," she greeted.

Gripping her elbows, she fixed her gaze on her boss.

"Ehem ... Mr Cookey, you remember my staff, Grace, the one that handled the promotion of ..." Her boss was all chatty.

"We have met on several occasions outside working environments," Morgan said, his eyes never leaving her face. "Haven't we, Grace?" He clearly wasn't expecting her to answer that. "There are some things I would want you to have a look at as we progress on this deal," he continued.

"What are those things I have to look at?" She faced him. The smirk on his face made her sigh.

"You can sort that out in your office, Grace. He will come to you when we are done here." Her boss blew off the fog that was already building.

She hurriedly left the two men and walked to her office. After the horrible date, he shouldn't be looking for her. She exhaled through her mouth, hung her coat, and switched her A/C on.

"You have been avoiding me," he said, chest thrust out. He pulled the chair opposite hers and sat down.

"And what made you think that I am avoiding you?" she asked, pursing her lips.

"You are not picking my calls, and you have refused to reply to my text messages since the day I dropped you at your house."

Under normal circumstances, she would have considered him—a man that knew what he wanted and would do anything to get it was her kind of man.

Ken knew what he wanted. You didn't give him a chance, her conscience spoke.

"That was two days ago," she put in, leaning forward.

"And those two days have been like two years to me," he said, resting his back on the chair. "So, why are you avoiding me?"

"I didn't say I am avoiding you. I'm just busy with work."

"You are not good with lying, Grace. You can do better than this. Come on. You are too busy that you cannot answer your calls? Or reply to messages? I am not a kid, Grace. Come up with another excuse, not this one."

She didn't say anything for a while. Nothing she said would convince Morgan, nor would he understand if she told him she was in love with the man she had walked away from years ago.

"What are you doing here, Mr Cookey?" She rubbed her forehead.

"Oh ... Have we gone back to you calling me by my last name? No more Morgan? Anyway, I came to see you."

"You shouldn't have come. Ehm ... I will call you when I'm free," she said, tapping her polished nails on her desk.

She would never be free for him, and he would not bother her again.

*

Grace spent the rest of Friday night ransacking her wardrobe, looking for something to wear to the birthday she was supposed to be going with Ken, and eating potato chips.

The next morning, she woke up from the heap of clothes on top of her bed where she had sunk into and slept off, her empty box on top of the bed, the empty pack of potato chips on the table, and with the realization that she still hadn't figured out what to wear to the party. Only one option remained.

"Come over here, girl. Let's fix you up," Debbie said to her over the phone.

"Debbie, you are a lifesaver. I know you will have something for me."

She pulled over in front of the boutique thirty minutes later. After forty-two minutes of going through the collections, she walked out with a wine-coloured, V-necked, shimmering long dress that defined her figure perfectly, gold drop earrings, a necklace, and eighty-five-thousand-Naira debit.

"I heard about your divorce, couldn't believe it," Debbie said as they headed for her car. "Both of you were good together. Ken cherished you, as well. Whatever happened?"

Strange to reckon she hadn't seen Debbie or talked to her in four years, yet Grace had her eyes on a woman who was leaning on her car, periodically darting her eyes side to side.

She is waiting for someone.

Was it her imagination, or did the stranger's eyes flicker immediately after the name Ken was mentioned? Their eyes met. The woman gave her a knowing smile, which she acknowledged with a nod.

"Yes, it's unfortunate it had to go this way, Debbie. We were tired of arguing about my job and how busy I was. I couldn't stay and not give him what he wanted. I had to leave," she said.

Eyes still on the strange girl who had negotiated to the other side of the road with a phone to her ear, Grace groped in her handbag for her keys.

"So you are the person that walked out of the marriage?" Debbie accused.

"What would you want me to do, Debbie? I had to either become the wife he wanted and lose my job, or keep my job while he suffers," she defended.

"And you chose to hold on to your job and let a man as nice as Ken go?"

"I was scared! I didn't know what to do."

"So have you guys been in touch since then?"

"He is actually the guy I am going to the party with."

"You don't say! You didn't tell me! I would have taken my time to make you a queen!" Debbie screamed.

"You have already turned me into a queen and have emptied my pockets."

They both laughed.

She entered her car and was about to drive out when Debbie said to her,

"Make the best out of this party, Grace."

She nodded and drove out.

*

Chinyeaka watched her drive out. It was her—the woman in the picture, the woman he said he cherished. She had picked the photo from Ken's sitting room the night she'd gone to his house, a mistake he would ever regret.

My lucky day. A wicked glint crossed her face. Meeting her was by accident—or would she say, 'divine arrangement.'

With her vehicle number written and stuck in her pocket, she was ready for her next plan.

CHAPTER SEVENTEEN

Squeals, whoops, and hollers over soft music that could get any couple in a romantic mood. Ken combed the beautifully decorated hall with his gaze, searched the faces of women— heavily made up and plain-faced—all trying to outshine the other. Twenty minutes into the party, and she was nowhere in sight.

He got a glimpse of the celebrant who had turned and rewarded him with a smile. He returned the gesture and headed toward Mrs Adekola and her husband.

"Ken! Here you are. We thought you wouldn't make it," Mrs Adekola said, flashing her teeth, of which the front row was already gone. The old woman took him into a warm embrace.

"Happy birthday Ma," he said.

"My boy! How are you? I heard about your partnership with Virony," Mr Adekola said.

"Yes, sir," he said humbly.

"That is good! Congratulations!" They both shook hands.

"So, where is Grace?" Mrs Adekola asked.

He needed an excuse.

"She is standing over there," Mrs Adekola announced.

His eyes fell on her. Exquisite! She had her dark and soft natural hair out, held together with a band that gripped it into a bun. One of her features he couldn't get over—he had loved touching and curling his fingers in that vibrant hair, especially during lovemaking. His gaze roamed over her body.

"Perfect," he muttered to himself, sucked in air.

Their eyes met. She waved. He straightened his tuxedo and walked towards her, clasping and unclasping his wet palms.

*

Grace instantly knew he was staring even without her looking. She'd felt it with the hairs of her body. When she finally settled her eyes on him, her breath quickened.

Oh, God! She bit her lip, tapping her fingers on her purse. It wasn't going to be just a party for her.

"I will be the envy of every man here. You look so divine," he whispered, taking her in a warm embrace that left her breathless.

The scent of his cologne caressed her nostrils.

"You smell nice," she commented before she caught herself.

He smiled.

"You like it?" he asked, gave her a peck on the cheek, then stood back to survey her. "Divine."

His breath on her face, like a feather on her skin, made her flush.

"You know I love it," she answered.

Tonight, she was going to flirt shamelessly. She would forget about the past—the fear, the uncertainty that had kept them apart.

They walked hand in hand into the party.

"I am glad you came. It means a lot to me." He gave her a direct stare. "You know that, don't you?"

She felt her stomach knot as it did whenever he was close to her.

"Kay ..." she breathed out. "It's nice being here."

She had not felt this special for a long time. He was all over her, making subtle, seductive comments, deliberately straightening her dress, touching her hair, gossiping in her ear, and introducing her to everyone.

"I wish the night would not end," he said.

She was afraid to admit that, too. Every nerve in her stood at any slight brush of his hands. When he took her by the waist and moved her to the rhythm of the music, she collapsed on his muscular chest, allowing him to lead them both.

Time passed so quickly.

"I have to go, Kay."

He saw her to her car, turned her to him, and without warning, placed his mouth on hers. She threw her hands around his neck and pushed her tongue deeper into his mouth. She didn't want to pretend to be over it—the heat he ignited in her threatened to lick her up.

"Come home with me tonight, sweetheart." His lust spoke, and he took her lips again, drawing moans out of her.

"Kay …"

"Please, my love … Don't deny me." He searched her face. "Come home tonight. I want to make love to you." He couldn't even hide his desire—but neither could she. "I am dying to spread your legs and lick your wetness."

His chest rose with his heavy breaths.

She shouldn't be doing this. Tightening her lips, she tore away from him.

"I can't, Kay." She shook her head.

"Why? You want this as bad as I want it! Just this night, my sweetheart."

Was that what he wanted? Just to lay with her?

"It is not good for us, Kay. If we have to do this, we have to be sure it is just what we want and nothing more."

With that, she entered her car and drove off.

Grace drove with her mind awakened to the feelings she had long buried and only imagined. She unconsciously touched her swollen lips, where the taste of him lingered. She wanted more.

What if he wants more than just one night of pleasure? What if he wants me to stay permanently?

Will I be able to be the woman he will love again? I failed him before, I may likely fail again.

The car halted with a screech.

Oh, God! She still loved him, had never stopped. But she didn't know if she could live the life of a conventional wife again. Her career always meant so much to her, but the tingling in her vagina blurred all that. She would not be able to sleep without having his erection thrusting and stroking every part of her inner walls.

She did a U-turn. Tonight, she was going to be his whore. Just for tonight.

But she was wrong.

*

Ken dropped his car key on top of the table and sank on the sofa. Grace was fighting everything she felt for him, he was sure now. He scratched his head. How could she deny the fire he had seen in her today? What had he done to make her despise the memories they had made?

He allowed his mind to bring back the image of her at the party. She'd taken his breath away. She was everything—beautiful, and so fragile, like a piece of goldware.

He had forgotten they were separated the moment he set his eyes on her at the party. He was proud of his woman. All he wanted was to hold her in his arms and drink from her fountain of beauty.

Twice, she had caught him staring at her lips.

"What?" she had asked the first time.

"What is what?" he had asked her back, pretending not to know what she was talking about.

She had looked down with shyness. He never knew dark women did blush until he met Grace. Her colour was that of polished bronze, and like rich chocolate, she glittered.

"You are looking at me again, Ken," she had accused him once more, biting her lower lip in that sexy manner.

Was that deliberate? She knew it turned him on when she did that. It reminded him of her face when she did sit on him to ride his cock.

"What do you mean? Can't I look at a beautiful woman again?" he had defended himself.

"No! You were looking at my lips," she'd pointed out.

And she was right—he'd watched every movement of her lips. "Your lips are making me lose concentration. They are beautiful."

He heard his gate open, and a car drove in. His gateman spoke to someone. At first, he thought Edu had come to bother him with Premier League stories, but when he peered through the window, he saw Grace walking towards the door.

His pulse raced as he hurried downstairs to open the door even before she knocked.

"Kay … I … I … thought I could come over to help you do some paperwork since tomorrow is Sunday and I don't go to work on Sundays."

The only words he heard was his name and 'Sunday.' He took her by the waist and led her inside, closed the door, and leaned on it. He watched her saunter like a queen inside the sitting room. She turned, and her brows creased with a frown.

"You don't want me here, do you?" she asked. "I can leave if you don't want me. I … just thought I could help you with some of your work tonight," she stuttered.

Ken knew she was lying. Her eyes betrayed her.

"Grace, you know I may not be able to stop myself from making love to you tonight," he said, not wanting to hide his feelings for her any longer. When she said nothing, he continued. "I want you so much that I can't pretend that you are not here with me and go to bed." His eyes narrowed as desire consumed him. "I want to touch you. To thrust deep into you and have you hold my head while I am doing that."

She closed up. "I don't want you to pretend that I am not here. I don't want you to stop yourself from touching me, Ken. I want you."

He grabbed her, crushing her against his chest.

"Sweetheart." His breath fanned her face. "You don't know how long …"

He bent his head and allowed his tongue to quench its thirst. She welcomed his mouth, gave, and he took. He offered, and she accepted, as well, then he pulled away to look at her eyes.

"I hope you know what you are asking for, my love."

"One more night with you is what I ask for, Kay."

He wasn't satisfied with just one night. He had wished she would say 'forever,' but he could manage what she was ready to give, and pray she accepted his offer later.

His palms skimmed down her shoulders, pulling her clothes from her body while he planted kisses on her ear, neck, and shoulder. He lifted her up as she wrapped her legs around him, placed her against the wall, teasing, tormenting her with desire and want. He ran his tongue on her nipple. She moaned with pleasure. When he stroked the beads on her waist, she went wild.

If all she wanted was just a night, then, an unforgettable night it would be.

So he carried her upstairs, to the bedroom they'd once shared, and on the bed that was filled with passionate memories of both of them. He spread her legs, planted feather-light kisses on her vagina lips, and she shuddered. When he sucked on her bud, her hands were on his head, pushing him deeper.

*

That same night, Chinyeaka lay naked on her bed, with the picture of the man that had tormented her dreams on her chest, her legs spread as she worked her fingers up and down her honey pot.

She imagined his fingers on her, his tongue on her breast, his moan as he rode inside her, her buttocks bouncing against his balls as he took her from behind.

She moaned his name as she pleasured herself, begging him mentally, calling him, offering to him what every other man would have wanted.

She pulled her fingers from her wetness, brought the pillow close to herself, legs wide apart to ride it, and placed Ken's picture in front of her. She rode the cushion as she would have done him, let out a loud moan, and her legs vibrated vigorously in a convulsive manner.

She looked at the picture once more. Hot tears gushed out of her eyes. She was obsessed with him and also hated what he made her do.

She vowed to make sure he knew no other woman except her, no matter what it took.

*

"Hello, I thought you wouldn't call again," Kola said with relief. Beautiful women had always made him nervous, especially when he seemed to be drawn to one.

He hadn't intended to fall for Imelda; he couldn't help it after he had enjoyed her company the second and the third time they had met.

"Sorry, I was waiting for a free time to talk to you," she replied.

It had been a long time since he'd stayed awake at midnight just to speak with a woman on the phone. But the new feeling welling inside him for Imelda was capable of making him break his own rules. He was going to ask her to be his girl—that was worth waiting for.

"Are you free now?" he asked her.

"I guess so ..."

"We need to talk, Imelda. When do we next see each other?" he asked and sensed she had tensed.

"What are we talking about?"

"I can't tell you over the phone ... Please, can we meet? I want to see you again."

"I don't know, Kola. It's going to be difficult this time around."

"Why?" He couldn't understand why she could not get herself to see him. She had been eager for them to meet some hours ago—she'd said so herself. "I can't wait to sit with you ... so fun to be with." Or was she only patronizing him? "Okay, can I come over to your place to see y—"

"No, no, no ... Please don't come," she cut in.

"What is the problem? Are you staying with your parents? I can introduce myself to ..."

He was still talking when he heard the voice of a man in the background, and then he heard her scream, a male voice shouting, and the phone went dead.

CHAPTER EIGHTEEN

The slap was unexpected. Imelda staggered, and the pile of boxes prevented her from landing with her shoulder on the floor, phone in her hand. She fell, and it shattered on the ground.

Ahmad could not stand her treating him like he didn't exist. For two days, he had tried to win her back to himself, had gone out of his way to please her. He had even borrowed some money from Kabiru yesterday to buy her a new pair of shoes which she'd just thrown beside the bed without even trying it.

He had endured her silence, had suppressed his anger when she'd turned down his offer to take her to his popular joint with his guys, and had even swallowed his pride when she'd turned him down in the night.

"Me, Ahmad, begging a woman for her pussy, and she was Queen of Sheba for me," he had complained to Kabiru.

He always cringed whenever he remembered how he was crawling to her like a little puppy, begging for her to open her legs. Yet, she denied him.

He had suspected she was seeing another man, but he had no evidence and wouldn't want to lose the chance he had to win her back. He had wanted to continue with the pretence but had already gotten to his boiling point.

"She has no fear for me again. She leaves the house and comes back anytime she likes," he had lamented to Kabiru.

"O boy, it's like another man is eating the pussy o. That's the only thing that could give her such boldness,"

Kabiru had replied, drawing a huge cloud with the smoke from his cigarette.

He hadn't wanted to believe it, but he couldn't come up with a better explanation of why Imelda had changed so suddenly. That night had been the last straw—she had ignored him in bed and was busy slurring on the phone.

But what happened next shook him to the bones …

*

Imelda could swear she saw a blackout and some stars dancing in the darkness with that slap. Then it was as if a nut was unscrewed from her brain, transforming her into someone she would never have imagined she would be if in her right senses.

Without thinking, she lifted her hand, and it landed on Ahmad's cheek. She saw his jaw move, and she could count her fingers on his cheek.

Ahmad was frozen. He looked at her like he would a raging madwoman. Blood rushed to face and surely turned it red, her eyes flared, and her breath was as heavy as the sound of a big armoured tank.

"Are you mad! You dey craze! How dare you raise your hands again on me?" She was screaming at the top of her voice. "All these years … All these years, Ahmad, I have fed you, clothed you, lied because of you, fucked you, lost friends because of you. I have lost my personality because of you. I don't even know who I am anymore …"

She was a breath away from him, daring him, looking him in the face and poking his chest.

With his mouth wide open, he sat on the bed, his bulging eyes resting on her.

"… I have been humiliated. I have lost my dignity searching for jobs for you … What do you do? You go out to drink with your guys and come back to practice your boxing with me," she continued.

"Imelda, you realize who you are talking to?"

Her sudden outburst seemed to have weakened him.

"Shut up! Shut the fuck up! Who you be? Who are you, Ahmad? What else can you do to me? You have used me, abused my body, ripped me with your constant demand for money, deprived me of love ... What else will you do to me? Hit me again? Okay, come on. Hit me! Hit me again, Ahmad! And I will show you that you are not the only one that has madness in his DNA. I will slice you with a knife and go to jail!"

She fled before he could recover from the shock. Scared that he may descend on her if she remained in the house, she left wearing just her nightwear for the second time.

She saw the peering eyes of her neighbours on her when she came out, the crooked smile on her landlady's face. She walked briskly out of the gate, then she ran. Her breasts bounced up and down, her slippers splashed drops of sands on her heels, but she cared little about her look.

She was able to enter a taxi. Most of the passengers looked at her with questions in their hearts, but none said anything to her. The tears were flowing freely by the time she got to her Madam's house, but she was disappointed when she met her gate locked.

*

Kola opened the door and saw her standing there. With no words, he took her in and sat her down on his sofa.

"What happened? Why are you like this?" he asked as he settled beside her.

"I gave him everything, and he gave me nothing. I was his meal ticket. He battered my body and my soul," she said, and then she turned to him. "I am the fool, you know, thinking he will change, that he was only frustrated because he has no job. I thought I could make him better ... Yes, I am a fool. I have always been a fool."

He said nothing. He didn't know how deep the cut was; he could only understand that this woman in his sitting room was on a long journey of self-realization and healing.

"You ... do you think I am a fool, too?" she asked him.

"No, you are not." He wanted to hold her hands but decided against it. He sighed instead. "You are a woman who was in love with the wrong guy."

Whoever this guy was, he must be the dumbest dickhead to ever walk the Earth.

When she finally calmed down, he carried her to his bed, covered her up, and closed the door behind him as he moved to the guest room to have a restless night.

*

Ken woke up to the arms of a woman around him. He'd almost forgotten that Grace loved to cuddle. They had joked about her love for cuddling and had named her 'Cuddly Bear.'

His gaze swept over her naked body and rested on her breasts. The way they rose and fell with the rhythm of her breath fascinated him. Her nipples—large, dark, and hard ... He caressed them gently, and she responded by snuggling closer to him.

He loved having her in his arms and in his bed again. He wished she would stay, that they would agree to make this work. He was ready to give her another chance and may even accept some conditions.

Ken inhaled. This is how it should be every morning. He gently removed her head from his shoulder, left the bed, and whistled down to the sitting room. He picked her phone where she had left it, fumbling with it. He wanted to open it, and when he finally did, one name kept appearing in her inbox.

Morgan

*

The ray of the sun filtered into the room and permeated through her eyelids. He wasn't there when she opened her eyes, yet his scent lingered, mixed with the odour of the previous night's passion.

Grace pulled his pillow close and sniffed. She took her time, enjoying it at leisure. Last night while Ken had made sweet love to her, it was as if the whole room had been lit up and the voice of a thousand orchestras made sweet melodies for them.

She stood up from the bed, covered herself with one of his shirts before going downstairs.

She saw him at the dining, watched him go through his records for a while before she came to him.

"Good morning, Kay," she greeted.

"You are awake! Good morning to you, my babe."

"Please stop calling me that, Kay. I am no longer your babe," she argued with that husky tone that came with mornings.

"You were last night. Are you regretting last night, Grace?" He turned to face her.

She smiled down at him "No, Kay. I am fine."

"Good," he said, handing her phone over to her. "You left it on top of the sofa. Meanwhile … one Morgan sent a message to you," he said casually.

Grace opened her mouth and closed it. She should get angry, ask him why he'd gone through her phone. Same thing he had done and found out about the IUCD. What was he checking?

"Ehm … hmm … it's not really what you think. He is just a guy I met …" All of a sudden, she felt the need to make him understand.

"Grace, stop, please. You owe me no explanation. It is your choice to make, but whatever your choice is at the end of the day, don't forget that I love you, and will wait for you. Just let me know when you decide to finally move on without me," he said, caressing her cheek.

A sob escaped from her throat. She felt little and unworthy of him.

"Last night was the best night I have had since you left, and you know the best part? I could tell you have not been with any other man since you left me, and it gives me a little hope. I will cherish what you gave me last night and will wait for you to see how much I want you back."

"Kay … How can you be this good? How can you easily forget what I did to you? How can you be so perfect? It's unfair."

"Let's just say I know what I want, and will not want the pain of yesterday to deprive me of you."

CHAPTER NINETEEN

Imelda pulled herself up from the bed and brought her feet down. Her breath caught sharply as the ceramic-tiled floor gave her an icy bite. She curled her toes, gradually introduced them to the tiles, which were friendlier this time. The room was beautiful and smelt of freshness. Nothing like hers that was stuffy and smelt of perspiration and tobacco.

She picked one of the books scattered on the table, scanned the blurb, and neatly arranged it with the others. On the wall close to the window was a pencil drawing of a beautiful lady with a warm smile. Maybe his wife? Her face creased with a frown—he would have mentioned that he was married. She pulled her eyes away.

She had slept well, something she had not done for a long time. She gasped at her reflection in the mirror that hung on the wall close to the wardrobe. Her hands flew to her cheek. She looked terrible, her eyes swollen, lips dry, stains on her face. She had a nightgown on, and she didn't know where it came from.

Her fingers traced the red marks on her cheek. Memories of last night came flowing back. The fight she'd had with Ahmad, her outrage.

Imelda gazed so hard at her reflection, in a moment, the woman staring back at her came alive. Both of them burst out laughing until tears ran down their eyes.

"You will no longer hold on to what was never there. It is time to look at life and see how beautiful it is," the woman said.

"I will no longer hold on to what was never there … I will no longer hold on to what was never there …"

She repeated those words, over and over again while walking towards the bed. She lay back and sank into a deep, peaceful sleep with those words on her lips.

*

She was still asleep when Kolawole got home at noon, the breakfast he'd kept for her untouched. He checked her temperature with the back of his hand, the way he had seen women do. She stirred and opened her eyes.

"Hey," he said.

"Hey," she replied and sat up. "How long have I been sleeping?"

"Since morning, I guess" he replied, smiling at her.

"I am sorry for inconveniencing you. I didn't have any other place to go to. My boss—"

"It's fine. I don't mind having the presence of a lady here after a long time," he cut in. "You didn't eat your breakfast."

"I didn't even know there was breakfast. I'm sorry. Please don't dispose of it. I will still eat it," she said, allowing him to hold her hand.

He stroked her pale hand, touched her face. "I left a note for you on top of the table."

"I'm sorry, I didn't check." Her voice came out, barely a whisper.

"That is okay. I understand."

He took his hands away. There was so much he wanted to know, questions, things about her, but he didn't want to scare her.

"You … you … undressed me last night." Hands curled around her middle, she avoided his eyes.

"Ehen … yes … But I didn't see much. It was dark anyway, and nothing happened. I didn't take advantage of you …" he defended himself.

"I know, don't worry. Not that it would have mattered if you had. Isn't that what every guy wants?"

He didn't answer her. He stood up and was about to leave the room. "The nightwear belongs to my cousin that comes here once in a while, and there is a cloth on top of the chair. It also belongs to her. You can manage it for now."

"Kola," she called out to him.

"Hmm?"

"Thank you."

"It's okay. I will go warm the egg sauce and bring it here for you while I boil rice," he said and walked out.

*

The best weekend ever. Ken grinned as he walked back inside after she'd driven out, whistling a tune, feeling happy and uncertain at the same time.

"I have missed you so much, Kay." She had held his head and breathed those words into his ear. "I think about you all the time."

He had tried to avoid bringing up the issue of her coming back to him permanently, at least not this weekend. He also didn't want to discuss Morgan. All he wanted was to have her with him, her undivided attention, and he had it.

"Don't forget to call me whenever you need me," she had said.

"I will be calling you every day until you will have no other option than to move in here," he had said, holding the car door for her.

She'd said nothing, but she'd allowed him to plant a lingering kiss on her lips before she drove off.

*

Grace was humming Yemi Alade's 'How I Feel' as she slotted her key into the keyhole. The stench of rotten food greeted her immediately as she entered her house. She wriggled her nose.

"My punishment for having too much fun," she said and emptied the pot in the dustbin.

Back in her room, her hand on her lips and a grin on her face, she reminisced on the sweet moment with Ken. He had taken her breath away.

"I like the way you move your body when I do this," he had said while teasing her clitoris with his tongue, his eyes on her face.

"You are wicked!" She had always told him this whenever he tormented her with pleasure.

"I like tormenting you like this," he would reply.

I love you, Kay …

Having sex with him hadn't quenched her longing. She had thought it would at least make her feel better, but now, she felt lost. She wanted what they had before, what he was offering—forever. However, she didn't see that happening, not with the edge between them.

She shook her head with sadness. She had yet another promotion coming up by the end of the year, and she knew what Ken asked for. Commitment. This may involve slowing down on her career.

"I have a company now. We can build together," he had said.

"Kay, it is not the same …" had been her reply.

She packed her hair up, removed her clothes, and unhooked her bra. She admired her breasts in the mirror, caressed one of her nipples—she could still feel Ken's warm mouth on it. She allowed herself a fleeting smile before sliding under her duvet to have a very long sleep.

*

Chinyeaka came out of hiding, legs heavy and numb, like a thousand ants were marching inside them. A wicked glint crossed her face. Situations had always turned for her good. She hadn't set out to stalk the woman—just a casual, secret visit to her dream man—as she had always done, and there she was, nodding and smiling at 'her man' while driving out from his compound.

She slept with him? Chinyeaka had waved down a tricycle and had followed the woman to this place.

She limped, clapped off sands from her palm, gave the house another glance, and walked off.

CHAPTER TWENTY

"Are you sure you will be okay?" Kola asked Imelda.

They had talked on Sunday night extensively. It wasn't in his nature to judge, so he'd tried to understand why she held onto a man who had manipulated and abused her for years.

"Ahmad was the only person who looked after me when no one wanted to," she had told him. "I was a fresh, poor, and naïve student who didn't even know where her next meal would come from. I was able to pay my first hostel fees and school fees but had nothing else with me. My hostel mates mocked me a lot, and you won't blame them. I had been eating from them for a long time, borrowing from them. They couldn't take it anymore."

She was sipping the ginger tea he had made for her, said she had not tasted it before but had heard it was good for the health. When he asked her about her parents, she frowned.

"My father abandoned my mother after she had a third child, which turned out to be a girl. He was desperate to have a son, someone to keep the family name alive. Before my mom came back from the hospital, Dad had moved out ..."

She had placed the cup on top of the side stool next to her, pulled her legs closer to her chest, and continued.

"We later heard that he already had a woman who had a son for him, and he had moved in with his new family ... My mum couldn't renew the rent, so we moved out of the flat. We couldn't go back to the village, either.

We were not welcome there, nor did my mum want to go back to her people. So at seventeen, my mum had already started wishing that I got married to ease her burden. You can imagine how she felt when I told her that I wanted to go to university."

"So how did you meet Ahmad?"

"I met him in a food joint. He came with his friends to eat and noticed I couldn't pay for my meal." She shrugged. "He paid off my old debt and bought food for me. We kicked off from there. I knew he was into something, not so good in school, but … I couldn't leave him. He was my only means of survival in school." Her chin dipped down, eyes going distant.

The conversation had gone from sad to funny, and they had laughed at some point.

"Are you a detective interrogating me?" she had asked him, and they'd both laughed.

"I couldn't leave Ahmad, can't you see? I didn't want to be termed ungrateful, after what he did for me." She'd tried to make him see her reasons.

"And now ..." he'd asked.

"I am done. I can't continue with him. He knows I have tried. It's time to move on."

She'd told him that she would put up with her Madam until she was able to get another apartment. He'd offered her his place, but she'd politely refused.

"What will you tell your girlfriend or your wife if she comes and meets me here?"

"I am single. My girlfriend left because she couldn't tell her family that her fiancé is a cook." His gaze was fleeting. "A fat cook," he'd added, and laughter had erupted from her mouth.

He loved the way she laughed over every little thing he said.

She had arched her eyebrow and chuckled. "Are you serious?"

*

"Ife mi, Ayanfe mi jowo ma fi mi sile. Mo se ileri fun e pe ma yi pada please don't go. How do I survive without you? I promise you I will change. I will turn a new leaf. I will get a job and will take care of you ..."

Ahmad followed her around as she packed her things.

"It's me, Ahmad, your babe," he whimpered like an abandoned child. "My love, please don't leave me ... I will do anything for you."

Imelda stood there, motionless. He held her legs, hid his head in between her thighs, bathing her with his tears.

"Babe mi, sanu fun mi, mo nife re, have pity, please. All those things I did to you were the work of the devil, ise Satani ni please my queen, you are my everything. Don't leave me now that things are difficult for me ..."

Kolawole walked in. He stood by the door and watched them, cast her a long glance.

"It's either now or never," he said to her and was about to leave.

"Is it because of him?" Ahmad sprang to his feet in anger. "This fat pig?" He pointed at Kola with disdain. "Look at him! A bloated balloon! What can he do for you, Imelda? Can he last five minutes on top of you? You will run back to me in a week!"

Kolawole turned back, rested a cold gaze on Ahmad. "No wonder she is leaving you. You are so pathetic," he said and walked out of the sitting room.

Ahmad hurried to her side, clutching her arm. "I am sorry for all I did to you ... but please don't follow this man. He will not treat you the way I do ..."

She looked down at Ahmad who was looking up at her hopefully. Suddenly, he became so little, his large eyeballs held her gaze for a while.

"You are right, Ahmad. He will not treat me the way you did." His eyes warmed up with hope. "He is treating me better, and you know what? He is a better man than you would ever be in your miserable life."

She pulled her legs from him. He crawled behind her as she walked out and shut the door.

She met her landlady fetching water on her way out.

"Imelda, are you back?"

"Iya, I will not be staying here anymore. Thank you for accommodating me all these years," she replied.

"Ah-ah! Just like that? Where are you going to stay? Ehem ... who will be paying me rent?" her landlady asked.

"Ahmad will pay the rent from now on, except he wants to move out, too."

She allowed herself to sob in the car. Kola did not stop her.

"You did the right thing," he said.

At some point, she had almost given in to Ahmad's plea—she would have changed her mind had he not followed her.

"Kola."

"Hmm?"

"Thank you for helping me do this."

He gave her hand a gentle squeeze and nodded.

*

Startled, Chinyeaka squealed and jumped up and down, allowing the offending rat to escape. A new job, a unique experience in another shithole. The job came with the house; she should at least be grateful. But she wasn't—the only thing she was thankful for was getting away from her cousin who would have dragged her into wretched thinking and mediocrity had she not left. She hung her bag on the protruded nail on the wall and threw herself on the foam.

She had taken the job to work as a waitress for an Ijebu woman, doubling as their maid. She had moved in with them in their three-room apartment.

The pay wasn't much, seven thousand a month, but it came with feeding, a place to lay her head, and if she played her cards well, more money in her pocket. She saw how Baba Ademola looked at her the day she came to apply for that work and how his eyes had followed her whenever she walked by. She knew it wouldn't be long before he would start coming to her for knacks, and she would grab the opportunity to make more money for herself. She made sure she moved around the house without any underwear to make her buttocks flap up and down while she walked past him.

Opportunity to make more money, which is what it was for her, but her mind was still set on winning Ken back. Besides, Baba Ademola would be helping her ease the sexual tension Ken had brought in her life.

The only thing she missed working in this new place was Ken. Not able to see or know what was going on in his life knotted her stomach, and her cousin knew nothing—she hardly left her salon, so it was useless counting on her.

Later that day, she would call one of Ken's sales girls and get the information that Ken no longer came out regularly.

CHAPTER TWENTY-ONE

"You are pregnant!"

Grace was sitting in her office that Thursday morning, wasn't in the mood to do any work at all, just moping at nothing. Those words from her doctor kept her weak. Oh, God! How could she have allowed this to happen?

"How?" She knew what a stupid question she'd asked when the doctor had looked at her, lips widened in laughter.

"I should be asking you that, ma'am. When you came here to remove the IUCD, you said you are no longer with your husband, and it was no longer necessary, so ..."

"Yes, yes, yes ..." She didn't want to be reminded continuously. She had known that with the way she had been nursing sexual feelings for Ken, one day, they would end of having sex, but she hadn't bargained for a baby!

"... I know you to be a cautious woman. When I saw your result yesterday, I thought maybe you just wanted to have a child," Doctor Harts had been saying.

Yeah, right. God must be laughing at her now. Running away from marriage commitment, now this? Who wanted a child on the eve of a double promotion? She'd tapped her fingernail on her teeth.

"Thank you so much, Doc."

He had walked her to her car. "I think you should keep it, Grace. You may not know the miracle a child could bring."

What was wrong with everyone? Get back together... don't make another mistake ... now a miracle coming out of a pregnancy she didn't plan for ...

She had nodded and driven off to work.

Grace tore off a piece of tissue, wiped her face, and blew her nose. I am so foolish; what was I thinking? How come it hadn't occurred to both of them to use protection? She hissed when she remembered she did not go around with protection in her bag. And Ken? Well ...

"God! How could I be so blinded with the passion that I forgot to ask him?" she mumbled under her breath.

And Ken should have known, or did he deliberately skip it? Was it his plan to make her pregnant and get her back to him? That explained it all.

"He wants to leave me with no option, to spite me, so I can come crawling back to him on his terms," she muttered.

A soft knock came, then Imelda walked into the office. "I want to know if you need anything, Ma."

"I am fine, Imelda." She sniffed, voice trembled.

"You have not eaten anything," Imelda pointed out.

"I really don't feel like it."

"But you have to eat some ..."

"What is it? Do you realize that I am not a kid, and I am capable of taking care of myself?" she snapped. "If I say I don't want to eat, then that is it. Don't talk to me like I am under your care."

She regretted her outburst immediately.

"I am ... I am sorry, Imelda." She took in air and exhaled deeply. "It has not been a good day, but it is not an excuse for me to take it out on you."

Her lips quivered, and she jerked to her feet, sending the chair rolling back until it hit the wall. Face covered with her hands, she broke down in tears.

"Is it what the doctor said?"

Grace nodded.

"What is it? What did he say to make you cry like this?" Imelda held her hands tenderly.

"I can't tell him that I'm carrying his child."

Not now. Until she had secured her promotion, what would happen if Ken knew she was with a child, his child!

She shut her eyes and shook her head. "No, Imelda, he mustn't know."

She was scared.

"What do you mean, you can't tell him you are with his child?"

She didn't want to talk about it, only wish it away—that is, if it were possible. But Imelda would probe until words slipped out, so she had to talk about it.

If Imelda was shocked when she heard about the pregnancy, she didn't show it. She sat there like a secondary school teacher would listen to her student and allowed her to pour out her heart.

"I don't want him to think that I am imposing the pregnancy on him. He may not even want it."

"But he wants you."

He had always done—he'd said so. And it hurt her so much that she had to come to this point in her life again. Why couldn't she have everything she had ever wanted? She wanted him, this child, and her job.

"Nobody said you shouldn't keep them all," Imelda said.

She shook her head.

"It's not that easy …" Imelda wouldn't understand her fears. "I don't think I can be a good mother to this child. Then I would leave the responsibility to him. He would complain like my father did and …"

She didn't want to turn out like her mother, who had lost both her career and her marriage and who had remained a sad woman since then.

"We may not know what he would make out of this news if we do not let him know. You cannot deny a man the joy of knowing he is about to be a father."

What would happen after the excitement of the pregnancy died down, and she was expected to be there when she needed to be somewhere else?

"Do you love him?" Imelda asked her.

"Hmm?" Grace had not been expecting that question.

"Do you love this man, ma?"

"I have never stopped loving him, but that is not enough, right? Love is not enough … It was not enough for us before. It may not work now."

"What are you afraid of?"

She broke down into sobs again. "I don't think I can do this. I may not even like the child when it comes."

He wanted marriage, a long-time commitment. She might fail again if she agreed to this.

Imelda embraced her. It was one of the best feelings she'd had that day. She threw her head on Imelda's shoulder and wept.

"I am so scared, I don't know what to do. I don't know how to be a mother. I have never been close to carrying babes. I don't even know what to do with this baby or myself … I don't know how to play the role of a wife, either. I'm terrible!" she wept.

"No, you are not. You have been an amazing boss to me, an amazing friend to Mary and me, a good asset to the firm, and recently ... a counsellor and a sister to me," Imelda assured her.

"That is all I am. My life revolves around work. I am useless to the world aside from business and sealing of deals."

"Don't say that, Ma. You are a treasure to those around you. That is why Mr. Ken cannot let go of you. He saw what he wants in you."

This made Grace smile. She pulled herself straight, wiped her eyes and the mucus from her nose with the back of her hands. "I have been crying too much today. Sorry for bugging you with my wahala."

"It's nothing, Ma. You would have done the same for me."

Wasn't it funny how the ones you were supposed to nurse back to life turned around nursing you? She wasn't strong, after all. She hadn't felt vulnerable until lately.

"How old are you, Imelda?"

"Twenty-six, Ma."

She smiled. "Thank you so much, Imelda, and you can call me Grace when we are at home. Enough of me now, so tell me ... Who was the young man that brought you to my house on Monday?"

Imelda blushed.

"Hmm ... so soon?" Grace chuckled.

"No o o, there is nothing going on between him and me ... Yet ..."

"But I saw the way he was looking at you. I think he likes you. He has been calling me since that Monday o, asking how you are doing."

"He is a nice guy and a splendid cook, too," Imelda commented.

*

He grunted, held her arched backside tight, and convulsed with eyes rolled up his head.

"Babe you sweet die, you go kill somebody walahi," Baba Ademola said, panting heavily and fanning himself with his cloth.

Chinyeaka dislodged herself, grabbed a discarded cloth to wipe her body, and eyed his limp penis. Why did it look disgusting after the act? She turned her eyes away.

His own would not be disgusting—my Ken. His was the only one she would never get tired of seeing. She gave a fleeting smile.

"Babe I wish we can do this forever. Maybe I should marry you."

She eyed him. A few nights of fuck, and the old fool was already singing. Who wouldn't? Sex had always worked for her—the key to everything.

Only it didn't work for her Ken, but it will! Time … that was what it would take.

"Eh … sweet girl, what do you think … you and I, we are a pair, you know."

He was sex-starved; she'd known the first night they'd done it. Mama Ademola had gone to bed, and Baba Ademola had crept into her small corner like he had today. She hadn't been ready then but had seen an opportunity.

Earlier the previous day, he had snuck inside the kitchen where she had been dishing out pepper soup for a customer and had smacked her buttocks.

"Oooohhhmmmm … stop now. Madam may walk in." She'd feigned anger.

"She won't. Please let me touch you small," he had said.

"Abeg go, you that couldn't fulfil your promise to me, where is the four-thousand Naira I have been asking of you since?" she had asked.

He had searched his pockets, brought out some dirty notes, and handed them over to her. It was not complete, but it would go a long way. She had promised someone some money tomorrow.

"You will make it up before I allow you to lay with me," she had warned.

"No wahala, please let me touch your ass small now," Baba Ademola had said, fingers spread like the eight legs of a spider, and licking his lips.

The sex was very quick the first night—she felt nothing. But today had been different. She had willed herself to think of Ken while the man humped her. She'd felt something, had even been close to climaxing.

She stood up to open the window, her naked butt bouncing vigorously as she moved.

"You have to leave now," she told him.

"Why? Let's have another round," he said, reaching out to touch her breast.

She slapped his hands off. "Please leave. Your wife will soon wake up and will find her way to my room."

He left when he realized she was not ready to give him any more sex. He hung his cloth on his shoulder, his big stomach bouncing up and down like a huge balloon filled with water. He disgusted her so much.

"Mtcheewww," she hissed as he walked out of the door, picked her phone, and dialled a number.

"Hello, how far? Is she the only one in the house? Ehen … ehen … okay … don't do anything until I ask you to. Your money is ready."

The line went dead.

She dropped her phone and smiled to herself.

That night, after Baba Ademola had left, she masturbated herself to orgasm with the fantasy she had built around Ken.

CHAPTER TWENTY-TWO

"I am pregnant."

Fumbling with the chain on her leather purse, lips folded, Grace waited for him to say something. She had left the office earlier than usual to come to his place. "He has the right to know," Imelda had said. Well, that was what she was doing. "I am with your baby."

His forehead furrowed, eyes fixed on her face. Didn't he understand what she meant?

"What? Please sit down."

She didn't realize she had been standing since she'd walked into his house. Her news had wiped the grin he'd had earlier. He now ran his hand on his head.

"Sweetheart, please sit," he added.

One leg over the other, she avoided sitting beside him and collapsed on the sofa opposite his. He was staring at her, opening and closing his mouth. Was that a smile gradually building on his face? She knew it—he had planned this all along.

She shook her head violently, swallowed a sob.

"This won't work, Kay." Her face hardened. "I can't do this."

"What are you talking about?" He looked at her as if she were insane.

"I can't settle for this life ..." She saw him jerk his head up. "I can't be a mother, Kay." She wished he would understand. "I am trying to figure out my life, and ..."

She threw her hands up in resignation.

"You have been figuring out your life for the past four years, damn it!"

She was taken aback at his sudden outburst. He had not been this angry since she could remember.

"Selfish! That is what you are. What do you take me for? How could you even sit there and tell me about figuring out your life with my child in your womb?" His nostrils flared.

"You don't understand!"

"Make me understand!" he screamed back.

She held his hands, desperate to make him comprehend. "I can't become who you want me to become."

He removed his hands from hers, held her face, his gaze fixed on hers. "What do you think I want, Grace?"

She squeezed her eyes shut, grimaced. A sob escaped her throat.

"You want a mother for your children. Someone who would always be there when you need her." She sniffled. "I am not that woman, Kay."

Tears ran down her cheeks.

"Who I want is you, Grace," he said through clenched teeth. "I don't want some brainless zombie who would answer yes to everything I say. I want you! With this baby." His face softened as he looked at her stomach. "You can have your career. Just come home when you are supposed to." His voice mellowed. "If there is anything that confirms we are supposed to come back together, it is this pregnancy. I want you here, with me, Grace."

"That is the problem. I cannot come home to you all the time … I will not always be here."

"Bullshit!" He released her face and turned his back on her. "If you cannot see that all I have ever done is love you … I have tried to prove to you that you are everything to me, irrespective of who you think you are.

Grace, you belong here! With me ... and for Christ's sake, you can always be here if you chose to!"

"I don't want to hurt you!"

They would go through this again. It would start with him accepting her and all the baggage, then he would complain, and they would fight ... and separate again. She would leave him worse than when she'd met him.

He turned, covered the distance between them in two long strides, grabbed her waist. "You are hurting me already."

He pulled her to him. She gasped, and he covered her lips with his. Raging, rough, punishing. She was out of breath by the time he released her.

"If after many years of staying away, you still burn each time I touch you, then you have to reconsider what you are thinking of doing."

She flushed. He was right. She desperately wanted this man.

"What we feel for each other is not enough to build a perfect home, Kay," she whispered.

"I don't need a perfect home, Grace. I just need a home filled with love. And—" he stared hard at her, "—you are having my baby, Grace. It is time you asked yourself, 'What do you really want?' What does passion, love, mean to you? What do I mean to you?"

He gave her an intense stare. "I am tired, Grace."

Then he turned and walked upstairs.

*

She is pregnant.

The words were playing in Chinyeaka's head like a record on steady playback.

She hated the sound of it. She couldn't believe that he would spill his seed in that woman, making her carry a child for him, while she had begged for his attention.

She threw a ceramic plate on the kitchen wall, and it shattered, then she looked over her shoulder.

"He did this to me! After I have begged him to love me, to have sex with me so I can carry his child. He chose her!" She was furious.

She had been serving one of their customers when the news had come from a salesgirl she had been able to get to her side. "That my oga other woman don get belle, I hear when my Oga dey tell person."

Chinyeaka had met with the new salesgirl the day she had come to Ade Odun. She had pretended to be Ken's new fiancée, and the silly girl had believed her. Who wouldn't believe it? After the story she had formulated that went around the area, she had spent the last money she'd had to purchase a lovely gown and a cheap perfume just to look good and believable.

Lies came so easy nowadays—not that she had never lied to get herself out of some shit—but she no longer had to think hard for them to start flowing. She had told the girl to be on the lookout for any other woman that may come around Ken, and also to listen to every conversation and get back to her.

Alone, in the kitchen, she thought of how to handle the situation. Her pregnancy would foil a lot of things.

"Bitch," she muttered. "She can't be pregnant for him. Then both her and the baby must go."

*

"Kay!"

He didn't stop.

"Kay, please!" Grace squeezed her eyes tight as he slammed his door. "Kay, don't shut me out!"

Fingers clenched, she stomped and yelled. He was ignoring her. What did he want her to do? She collapsed on the sofa, covered her face, and cried. She had never felt so helpless.

Cries reduced to sobs, sobs into sniffles. She cleaned her face, pulse steadied, and decided to try again.

"Kay?" She gently pushed on his door, and it squeaked open. Her heart raced again. She suddenly had a new fear—losing him. "Kay, I am sorry."

She walked towards him. Every step made her heart pulsate faster.

"I thought you would be gone by now." His voice was raw from exhaustion, but without the edge that had been there earlier.

"I don't want to go." Her voice trembled. "I don't want to run any more. I don't want to lose you again."

She grabbed him from behind. His body stiffened, but she held on tighter.

"I am scared of becoming my mother or you becoming my father." His heart rose and fell slowly. "I love you so much, I was scared I would hurt you."

"Oh, woman." He faced her and touched a finger to a tear on her cheek. "Haven't you realized that you mean the world to me?" His hand circled around her waist, the other tipping her face up. "I have loved you like my life depended on it. Your parents made their choices based on the limitations of their knowledge then. It is ours to right the wrongs. Grace, you are not your mother, and we can work this out, sweetheart. Just don't walk away without trying. Will you do that for me, my love?"

She nodded.

"I will do anything you want me to do." She sniffled.

"I don't want you to do anything I want." He touched her nose, and she fluttered. "Silly small woman," he purred, voice low and sexy. "I want you to be who you are with our baby and me."

She nodded.

"Then, I will stay." She smiled broadly. "With you and the baby. Here or any other place you will call home."

"What of your work?"

"I will always go to work from here."

His eyes shone as he stroked her lips.

"Talking about doing anything I want you to do …" He smiled coyly. "I will want to make love to you, my little woman."

She bit her lip. The way he'd said it flooded her with sexual lust. "I would love that so much."

He brought his hand up her back and unzipped her gown. His fingers brushed her shoulders as he slid the garment off her. She shivered when he took her in his arms.

"You are divine," he said through her braids. "You make me want to explode with longing. I can never have enough of you."

His mouth lingered on her neck.

Her breath quickened, lips parted as he nibbled on her throat. His tongue found her ear lobe and gave it a gentle bite. The hairs on her nape rose, and she felt a warm sensation, a tingling between her legs that left her weak.

"Kay …" She lifted her chin, exposing her neck for him.

"Hmm." He brought his hand down to squeeze her backside.

"Kay …" she gasped. "I want …"

"Tell me, sweetheart," he murmured.

"I want you so much …"

He unhooked her bra, slid it off her, and lifted her. Propping her ass, she curled her legs around him.

"I don't know how long I can endure your torture," she said.

He chuckled.

"I love it when you beg," he murmured through the kisses he planted on her lips before he carried her to bed. "Not a bad idea, quarrelling and making up with sex."

She slapped his shoulder.

CHAPTER TWENTY-THREE

Chinyeaka stood in front of the gate with the package and looked over her shoulder. If today went without success, she would not be able to do this again. It was the second day she had waited. The first day, no one had come out of the apartment.

Settling for a particular plan had been difficult as she'd come up with a handful. Pay someone to follow her to her office and kill her. Her hitman could wait for her by five a.m. and stab her on her way to her routine running. Or pay someone to run her over with a car.

She had settled on poisoning. Yes! Using her passion against her. A gift from Ken would not be wrong, a guaranteed passage to her death.

It was difficult knowing which one would do. Someone like Ken would not give his woman a cheap wine. Chinyeaka had kept picking and dropping bottles. One of the attendants in the supermarket had watched her for a while and then approached.

"Excuse, ma'am, are you looking for a particular wine?" she had asked.

She had glanced at her and had shaken her head, told her she was making her choice, but she didn't leave her alone; she kept coming over to her side.

"I can help you make a good choice," she had offered.

"I am not blind, either! I know what I am looking for!" she had snapped. The poor girl had run.

Sales girls. Soon, she would no longer be addressed as such herself, when she would assume her rightful place beside her man Ken.

She had randomly selected one that cost almost all the money she had remaining. She was left with seven hundred Naira after she had paid for it, bought a gift wrap, and a cardboard paper.

She had sat down outside the supermarket to scribble the words, 'To the woman I love, from Ken.' She condemned half of the cardboard paper and was almost getting agitated when a young boy of about fourteen approached her.

"Can you make good calligraphy for me?" she had asked him.

"Yes, na, I can, but you will pay for my service."

The boy had done the calligraphic design, handed it over to her, earned himself a rumpled fifty Naira note.

She'd given out a wheezy breath. This wasn't as easy as she had thought. What if she got caught? Her gaze swept around the environment. The passers-by paid no attention to her, yet she trembled like a leaf in Harmattan. If the plan did work—and Grace drank from the wine today—then she would be dead and out of the way before morning.

What if she called Ken to confirm?

Chinyeaka frowned. She hadn't thought of that earlier. She, however, dismissed it. Love could make someone fool-headed; the woman may have taken the wine before thinking of calling her lover and would be dead before he got to her.

The boy that had handed her the poison had assured her that it would start taking effect a few minutes after the victim ingested it. That was why she'd chosen that night when she knew no one would come looking for her.

*

"Babe, don't keep this man waiting now. You have been in front of this mirror for like ages," Grace shouted at Imelda. She was as excited as the young girl.

"I want to be sure I look perfect," Imelda said, tilting her head to the left to view her cheek.

"It is past seven already, and you said you are meeting him in his place by seven."

"I know, but ... Okay, let me put the finishing touch to my hair."

"Girl, you look perfect. Your hair is nice. Can you just go?" Grace held her by the shoulder.

"I'm going already. So, how do I look?" Imelda asked, spun around.

"You look gorgeous. Oya go burst his head with your beauty but don't confuse him too much. Seriously, Imelda, this night is your night. Make the best out of it, enjoy it to the fullest, but don't be pressured into doing what you wouldn't want to do."

"Thank you, sis. You are just wonderful."

"You are just sweet, Imelda. So do I wait up for you, or are you sleeping over?" Grace winked.

"I will definitely come back, but ... if I can't, I will still let you know."

"Oya get out of my house now. Let me lock the door," Grace said, and they both laughed.

Imelda grabbed her purse. "You still owe me a gist."

The heels of her sandals clicked on the tiled floor as she hurried out.

"I promise to tell you everything." Grace smacked her buttocks. "Now get out."

*

The gate was flung open, and a lady walked out. Not the face she had been expecting—her informant hadn't told her someone else was staying in the apartment with Grace. Probably, this woman may have come for a visit, she thought.

"Excuse me? Who are you looking for?" the lady asked her.

"Ehem … I am looking for Aunty Grace," she stuttered. Chinyeaka felt like puking at the word 'Aunty.'

The lady gave her thorough scrutiny, turned her face back to the compound.

"Grace, are you expecting someone?" she shouted, with no reply. "And who do I tell her is looking for her?"

"I brought this gift to her, from my boss Mr Ken. He said he couldn't come by himself."

She was a natural! She should consider taking up a role in Nollywood.

The lady took it from her, weighed it, brought it closer, and read what was written. Her face softened with a smile. "My name is Imelda, I am her friend. I will give it to her."

Chinyeaka hesitated. "Is she at home?"

The lady squinted "Yes. Do you want to see her?"

"No … I want to be sure she receives this." She let go of the package, hurriedly walked away, praying that the lady she'd met would leave immediately and allow Grace to drink from the wine.

She didn't want both women dead. That would be too much and could raise more questions. It would become obvious they had been poisoned. But if only Grace got poisoned, her visitor could be held responsible. Hmm … genius! She hadn't thought of it this way, nor had she known that fate would aid her in this mission.

She looked over her shoulder before turning to the other street.

*

Grace walked back and stretched herself on the cushion. Imelda wanted a gist of how her yesterday's visit with Ken had gone. How would she tell without flushing all over? She bit her lip and smiled.

"Oh, Kay," she muttered, her hands crossing her middle.

When he had taken her to bed and started kissing her naked body, her mind had gone completely blank. Only one feeling had been left—spine-thrilling, vein-tingling sensation. He knew how to make her melt in his arms.

She stroked her body where his hands had roamed last night while his lips had trailed an erotic pattern down the hollow between her two breasts.

"Jesus! Grace, you are too beautiful," he had said. He had detached himself to tug on his belt.

"Let me," she had offered, and before long, his tan skin had glowed before her. And as he'd pulled her tightly against his body, she had felt the hard evidence of his desire.

Grace threw her head to the side, clamped her thighs together as she remembered how his warm mouth had covered her hard nipple and he had sucked, flicking his tongue up and down. She groaned.

"My Kay ...Why did it take me this long to realize?"

She adjusted her head on the arm of the sofa, wet her lips.

He was a patient, selfless man. With two of his fingers inside her wetness, he had given her pleasure until she'd exploded, gushing warm juice in his palm. He had entered her, his erection touching her walls, sending waves of pleasure.

"Grace o, you have a package!"

She flicked her eyes open and jerked up.

"From who?" she asked, running to open the door. Her eyes lit up as she examined the parcel. "Where is he?"

"Didn't come himself. He sent one of his sales girls. She said he would have been here but has been busy," Imelda said.

"Oh."

"You are glowing, Grace." Both ladies laughed. "I told you everything will work out fine."

"I know, Imelda. I know."

With the package clutched to her chest, she walked back into the house. She was experiencing love again—mind-blowing. Why did she even come back?

Give me a week to move in, she had told him when he had insisted she should stay.

"But we are no longer married," she had added.

"Who cares? We can remarry tomorrow."

She wouldn't want to be moving and still come here to pick one or two things, so a week he had given her.

Grace tore the wrap, read the label. Non-alcoholic. Nice. It wasn't a wine she knew him to drink. Change of taste, maybe. She sauntered to the fridge and brought a glass cup and a wine opener. Then she picked a plate of leftover fried potatoes and settled for a midnight movie.

CHAPTER TWENTY-FOUR

"You look beautiful tonight, Imelda."

She took his extended hand, and he walked her inside his house. It wasn't her first time there, but she noticed the special touch he had given to his sitting room, like the flower vase and a centre table that hadn't been there the last time she had been in the house. The whole place had the smell of lavender, and the light had been changed to a blue. He had her eyes on her, waiting for her approval.

"Your house is …" She gestured around the spot. "Thank you for doing all of these to make me happy." She felt bad for saying what she had said the last time. "I really didn't mean any of those words …"

"Yet, the house needed refurbishing." He blushed.

This made her laugh.

He blushed easily, with his cheeks pulled up like those of a cute cat.

"It's beautiful." Her eyelids fluttered.

His eyes lingered on her face. She looked away and cleared her throat.

"Oh, yes." He laughed awkwardly. "Come."

He sat her down and settled beside her, grinning.

Both hands on her lap, tapping, and giving him furtive glances, she burst out laughing when he kept shifting towards her and giving her glimpses, too.

"Sorry." He moved back, making her laugh some more. "I am sorry for making you uncomfortable, but … I don't know … You make me act like a child whenever I am with you. I seem not to know the right thing to do," he said, laughing.

"I don't mean to make you feel that way, either. I am sorry."

"No, don't apologize."

Her heart raced, waiting for him to tell her what it so desired to hear from him. She had planned her response if he properly asked her for a love relationship, didn't want him to wait any longer. She was eager to know how he felt about her.

They had been good friends for months, and she wanted something more.

"So how was work today?" he asked.

Really? She squeezed her eyes and opened them. How could she get him to open up?

He was more comfortable telling her about his plan to start up his own restaurant. Imelda knew he was battling with something to say. He kept stealing glances at her every now and then, smiling broadly.

"You are beautiful," he said over dinner.

When she caught him staring, she blushed.

"Amazing, as usual," she commented as she savoured the chicken pepper soup with white rice.

"Thank you. I am glad you like it."

Ahmad forgotten, she was ready for what this new man was prepared to offer. She wanted to be with him as long as he wanted. His smiles, his kindness, the way he treated her like a proper lady. She wished there was a way to show him what she felt …

"You are staring now." His spoon down, two hands supporting his jaw, his lips curled in a silly grin.

"You have not eaten much of your food, either?" she asked, aware she was looking at his lips. And he kept sticking out his tongue to lick those lips.

She joined him in laughing.

"You are an amazing cook. I don't think any woman can top you on that," she said, dropping her spoon and wiping her mouth with the serviette, glad they could talk about something else. She didn't know how long she could stay without striding over to him and covering his lips with hers.

"My mother was an excellent cook. Unfortunately, my sister didn't get that talent. I did."

"Your sister. Is she the person on the portrait in your room?"

"Yes. I made that portrait from the only picture of her I have. My parents burnt everything that reminded them of her after her death. That was before I came back from Italy."

"Sorry," she said, voice low.

"It's okay. It's been six years now. So what of you? Do you cook?"

"Yes, when I have the chance to. Not that I cook as good as you, though."

"I'm sure there are dishes you can cook that I cannot," he consoled her.

"I don't think so," she replied with a chuckle. "You can cook almost everything!"

They laughed like two school friends. He made jokes, and she laughed so hard until tears trickled down her cheeks.

"Oh my God, you are so funny. I can't believe you made me laugh this hard," she said, wiping tears from her eyes with the back of her hands.

This was where she belonged—with this handsome, shy chef. If only he could tell her he felt the same way.

*

Grace opened her eyes to the buzzing of mosquitoes and total blackout. She heaved herself up. The plate of potatoes, which was balanced on her stomach, rolled over and shattered on the ceramic floor.

She hissed, wiped the perspiration from her face with her palm, and stood up. She groped for her phone, tapped the touchscreen on, and looked at the time. Past ten.

I told Imelda that she may not come back, but she didn't believe me. She switched the television socket off, kept the TV remote on top of the table. This place is a mess. She avoided the shattered pieces of plate, and walked towards her room, saw the bottle of wine and the glass on top of the dining. Without much thought, she grabbed them. I can as well indulge while waiting for Lady Cinderella.

She sank her buttocks on the bed, scribbled a message to Imelda, and popped the bottle open.

"Your daddy wants us to celebrate." She stroked her stomach.

*

"I have not laughed this hard in a long while. Thank you so much for making me so happy this night," Imelda said.

"You look more beautiful when you laugh," Kola said to her.

There was an awkward silence, back in the sitting room. Her phone bleeped. She read the text and laughed.

"My Madam wants to know if I'm coming back," she said to him.

"Do you want to go? It's the weekend."

"I have to. She is alone, and you need to go to work tomorrow."

Please ask me to stay, Kola. I don't want to make a fool of myself. She liked how he made her feel.

"Imelda ... I have meant to tell you this," he started.

"Hmm?" Her heart galloped.

"I ...I ... I think I like you. Okay, it's more than that. I feel something more for you. I don't know if it is too early to call it love, but ... I want to be with you."

He looked at her. Her breath caught in her throat. All she wanted to say flew off her mind. All she wanted to do was throw her arms around him.

"I found myself thinking so much about you, but ... in a good way." He fiddled with his fingers. "I smile alone when I remember you. I imagine what it would be like to call you mine. I call you every time just to hear your voice ... So I ask, how do you feel about me?"

His eyes fixed on her, pleading, waiting.

She covered her mouth with her hands, swallowed a sob.

He frowned. "I am sorry, Imelda. I shouldn't have said that. I really don't want to hurt you."

She shook her head, sobbing. He didn't know how happy he had made her.

"No, Kola—"

"It's fine if you don't want me. Please don't cry."

He moved closer to her, held her hands and squeezed. He brought her palms to his lips and kissed them one after the other. A soft sob escaped her throat. It was so amazing to have him brush his lips on her palms like he did.

"I will wait for you."

"I think so much about you, too." She sniffed. It was a moment she had always dreamt about; she'd known it was love the moment he'd said those words.

"I don't understand."

"You asked how I feel about you, right?" She smiled. "Love. I love you, Kolawole."

Her heart swelled with excitement.

His eyes fluttered. He laughed and pulled her against him.

"You don't know how long I have kept this feeling to myself. Each time I see you, I lost words to say." He planted kisses on her neck and her cheeks. "I promise to treat you better, my queen."

When his lips sought hers, she held his head and took what he offered.

*

"Nice."

Grace savoured the taste of the wine. With sleep gone, and no Imelda to chat with, she sincerely wished she had heeded Ken's plea and had stayed. Loneliness was eating her up. She sipped again. Resting her head on the wall, she shut her eyes for a while and decided on something to do with her time. She dropped the bottle by the side stool beside the bed and went for her laptop. Just then, her phone rang.

"What is keeping you awake?" The phone on speaker, she switched her laptop on.

"What do you think?"

"I don't know." She wet her lips. Like the first time they dated, she felt like she was falling in love for the first time. "Work, maybe?"

"I don't work like you." The huskiness in his voice sent tingly sensations down her spine. "I am missing you so much." She heard him suck in air. "I wish you were here."

"What would you have done if I was there with you, Kenneth?" She put her laptop on the bed and pulled her legs up against her chest.

"You know what we would be doing now, don't you? You would have been paying for all those years you left me ... I would have made your whole body tremble."

She clenched her vagina and gave out a soft moan.

He laughed. "I know you want that."

"I just left you in the morning," she purred.

"What is wrong with a man wanting more?"

They both laughed.

"I got your gift. Thank you." She picked the glass and drained the remaining wine in it.

"Which gift?"

"The bottle of wine you sent to me." She smacked her lips.

"I don't have any idea what you are talking about."

"Ken, please be serious. You sent one of your sales girls here with a wrapped bottle of wine, which is adulterated, by the way. It has your name on it." She sat up straight.

"I am serious, Grace. I didn't send anybody to you, not to talk of giving you a bottle of wine ...Wait a minute. You said the wine was adulterated?"

"The cork looked like something that was tampered with like it was sharpened with a knife or something, and I thought it could be Aba version of the drink."

By this point, she started to panic.

"Jesus Christ! Grace, what does this sales girl look like?"

"I didn't see her. She handed the package over to Imelda and left."

She was scared now.

"Where is she now, I mean Imelda?"

"She has gone out for a date."

"You are alone?"

"Yes! And I have already drunk from it." She squirmed.

"Jesus Christ!"

"Ken ... Do you think someone ... Oh, no!"

"Grace! Calm down. It might be nothing. Maybe a friend trying to play some prank on you ..." She heard shuffling from his end. "I am coming over."

The phone went dead.

The first pang of pain hit her a few seconds after she'd dropped the phone. Her throat dry and itchy, her chest tightened. She felt her lungs being squeezed, gasped for air.

Grace rolled off the bed. That was how much she could fight before darkness overtook her.

CHAPTER TWENTY-FIVE

"My little woman."

Grace opened her eyes to see him smiling at her, gently stroking the back of her palm. She tried to move, but he gently pushed her back on the bed.

"What happened?"

"I thought I had lost you." He bent and kissed her forehead. "I have never been so scared in my life. I don't know what I would have done without you."

Her throat still hurt, and she felt a knot in the pit of her stomach each time she moved.

Realization hit her. She touched her stomach, eyes widened.

"My baby! Did I lose her?" Tears trickled down her cheek "Ken, did I—"

"Only one."

She pushed herself to sit. He supported her back with the pillow and rested her head on the bed's headrest.

"We are lucky, my love," he added.

Her eyes darted around, searching for more explanation. "What do you mean, only one?"

"They were two." He forced a bitter smile.

"Oh, Kay ..." She felt a lump on her throat. "I am sorry ... I am so sorry."

"Hey, it wasn't your fault. You are a strong woman. You fought to live."

She knew he was suppressing his own pain.

"At least I have you and the other baby. The doctor said you were poisoned," he continued. "By the time we brought you here, you were unconscious and bleeding."

She felt something was wrong—he wasn't telling her the whole truth.

"Are we going to lose the other baby?" she whispered, and he looked away. "Kay! Is the other baby okay?"

*

Ken didn't tell her that they may not only lose the other baby, but also her womb. She would be devastated and may decide to move on. After all, it was the baby that had made her want to stay.

"We have been able to come out of the life-threatening situation. The poison has been flushed from her system," the doctor had said. "Anyways, we may still be at the risk of losing the remaining babe, and we are yet to ascertain the level of damage done on the womb. If the result turns out bad, we may have no option but to evacuate the baby and ... depending on the level of damage, she may lose her womb ..."

"And there is nothing else you can do to save it?" he had asked.

"For all we know, her womb may be okay. Even the baby. I am just saying in case the result turns out bad."

He would not let her know, at least not now, not until she was strong enough to shoulder whatever the result would be.

As he looked at her now, so fragile, she was all that mattered to him. They could always make another baby or adopt one or two, but he wanted her alive and well. He stroked her cheek.

"The baby will be fine. Nothing will happen to him."

Even if something happened, he would still love her.

*

Leaning on a pavement in front of the restaurant where she worked, Chinyeaka fixed her gaze on the road while her mind wondered. She had never killed before, not even a goat! Her stomach tightened. Her limbs trembled, and her heart raced so fast immediately, she handed the package over. She shook her head—what if somebody had seen or followed her?

It had been a very long night. What she'd done haunted her, along with the fear of being caught. She wasn't in the mood to rumple the sheets with Baba Ademola. She was beginning to get fed up with his many demands, sweating while humping her like a stuffed duck. He disgusted her.

He had come to her as usual, but she had pretended to be fast asleep and had not opened the door. He had whispered through the keyhole, begging her to open. She hadn't even moved from her bed until she'd heard his footsteps down the corridor.

His son Ademola had come back from Togo the previous day, and with what she'd overheard them discussing last night, it seemed like he would not be going back any time soon.

She had run into him this morning when fetching water from the drum outside.

"Hoi beuriful laidi, jiu wek hio with ma mama?" he had asked her with a fake accent, speaking from his nose.

Getaway, you Bonkom! She would have loved to fire back at him, but she had something else occupying her mind now.

She wiped her sweaty palm on her apron. She wouldn't have gone that far, would have just scared her or something, but then would she have just walked away like that? Would Ken look at her with Grace still alive?

Her phone vibrated, and she nervously brought it out from her pocket.

"It has happened," someone said from the other end.

"Are you sure? Did you see her?"

"I saw them carrying her out. I think she is dead."

She cut the call, straightened her clothes, and walked back into the restaurant. It wasn't bad, after all—it was worth all the stress. She would start the journey of winning his heart when all this had calmed down.

Later that night, she would bring out his picture.

"I did this because of you," she would say. "I saved you from the spell that woman has on you, so you will be able to love me."

The picture would come to life. She would see him smile; she would take his hands and walk by the ocean where only they existed, no Grace, no Ademola nor his father, no filthy restaurant. Just him looking at her with adoration.

CHAPTER TWENTY-SIX

"When were you going to tell me about it?"

Grace turned her face away from him. She didn't want him to see how miserable she was. She didn't want him to feel sorry for her, either.

This was so unfair! Her lips quivered. How could she lose it? When she was beginning to love the baby, to feel the movements, the intimacy, she had lost them all. Those moments in the bathroom when she would stand naked, with the water trickling down her body, hands rubbing her stomach, she would speak to her. She had wanted the baby to be a girl.

"Imelda is preparing pepper soup this evening. Hope you will like it, little lady?" she would say to her little bump.

Tears rolled down her cheeks.

He had hidden the truth from her, had lied to her on why the scan was done, until today when she'd heard it from a nurse!

"Why did you have to lie to me about this?"

"To protect you, Grace."

Her anger choked her. She felt useless. She shoved his hands off as he approached to touch her. I don't want his pity. She couldn't face him. She should have died with the baby and forgotten about everything.

She was angry at herself—why did she even think it was worth the try? He'd made her love the idea of becoming a mother, and she had desperately wanted the baby to come, a gift to him, a proof to herself that she could achieve it.

"One moment, I was with babies. The next moment, they are gone! A dream, a mirage ..." Her voice trembled. She covered her face and cried.

"As far as I know, we still have a chance of saving the baby and your ..." He looked away.

"My womb! Say it, Kay." She sat on the bed. "Oh, God!" she exclaimed with her hand on her mouth. "Oh, my God!"

He'd said saving the baby. What baby? The nurse had said it wasn't breathing. Dead. A dead child in her stomach! And he stood there telling her about saving it.

He sat beside her, pulled her into his arms. She didn't stop him this time and sobbed softly.

"You shouldn't be crying now, so you don't hurt yourself. You need to recover," he said. "It may not be all bad. We still have hope."

A sense of failure overtook her.

"Why am I failing in the simplest thing every woman knows how to do? Why couldn't I keep my baby alive?" she sobbed.

She had let him down again.

He tightened his grip around her. "It wasn't your fault. I am responsible, too. Whoever did this may have something against me."

He was doing it again, masking his hurt. Maybe he was blaming her. This wouldn't have happened if she had not returned to her house as he wanted. He would have known how to protect her. Maybe she would have even called earlier enough when she got the wine. That would have prevented her from drinking it.

She still had her head on his hard chest when the doctor walked in. They gently disengaged. Eyes on the doctor, heart beating fast, she hoped for something good.

"It's good news, people."

She gasped, grabbed Ken's hands for support.

"I think the little one wants to live. He is breathing well, and you, ma'am, are okay, no organ damage."

"But … the nurse said he is dead!"

"Well, I am the doctor, and I am telling you what I saw."

CHAPTER TWENTY-SEVEN

"She is alive!"

Gut-wrenching anguish overtook Chinyeaka.

Life was so unfair. Why must she go through Hell to win a man? Yet, it had backfired. What had gone wrong? How was it even possible that she would be sitting in front of his car, both of them driving inside his compound?

Her breath came in short, wheezy draws. Beads of perspiration drew together on her neck and forehead to form thin streams that trickled down her body, soaking her clothes. She felt nauseous and needed to get more air before she would collapse.

"How is it possible?"

She covered her mouth, suppressing the scream that was about to erupt out of her. She had concluded that it would be a memorable day for her—she would no longer hide to watch him like before; she would walk to console him on his loss.

Speech rehearsed, acts well mapped out, she had envisaged a breakthrough. He would be vulnerable, 'and vulnerable men do irrational things,' her mother had said to her father once.

From the kiosk where she sat, she could see anyone approaching. Her gaze followed the couple until the gateman closed the gate. She paid the shop owner for the drink she couldn't finish and walked out. Heavy legs drawn in front of the other, bile rose to her throat. She could taste her own bitterness.

His gate closed, smashing her heart. Hot tears like angry storms rolled down her cheek. She felt the eyes of passers-by. She didn't care, dragged her feet, and willed her spinning head to focus lest she stumbled and completed the humiliation. She batted her lashes, shaking the wetness that stung her eyes. I will not cry. But before the hot tears slid down her cheek, she knew it was a lost battle. She turned and ran, wiping the mucus from her nose.

That night, she didn't wait for Baba Ademola to come to her. She went into his room and let her wrapper go. As he mounted her, she cried, allowing her pain and heartache to flow with the tears. She called him 'Ken' as he pushed in and out of her.

When she slipped into a deep sleep, the only face she saw laughing at her loss was that of Grace.

*

"Can't sleep?"

Imelda tore her eyes from the book she was reading and cast her gaze on him. They had not spoken much since the incident. Soaked in guilt, she had not noticed his pain, too. On the morning of the event, she had blamed him.

"I should have been with her. I shouldn't have listened to you."

He had allowed her to vent her frustration on him. Now she knew he had blamed himself, too—just that he didn't say it out or throw fists like she did. He leaned on the wall, with his loosed jogger and bared chest, arms crossed.

"Yes, I can't sleep, series of nightmares. I guess peaceful sleep is not for me for now," she answered.

He had insisted she stay with him after he had bailed her out from the police. A suspect for the attempted murder, she had spent two days in jail.

"The house will be lonely. Grace is not there with you," he had said when they'd left the station.

He eased himself off the wall and walked towards her, stood behind her, and gently took the book. He scanned the back cover and handed it over. "That makes the two of us. I couldn't sleep, either."

"So what was keeping you awake?" She had missed him so much.

"Many things." He took the space beside her.

Her eyebrows gathered in.

"I am sorry, Kola." She shifted so her body could touch his, wanted to take his hands but decided against it. "I was mad at you for nothing. I shouldn't have blamed you."

Her chin quivered, and she lowered her gaze.

"I am not angry at you, Imelda. I should have listened to you when you said you wanted to leave. It was selfish of me to keep you here."

But he hadn't kept her—she had wanted to stay. Just that, she sighed, it was wrong timing.

"You are not selfish, Kola. You didn't force me to stay." Her eyes watered. "I have put you through a lot since I came into your life. Kola, it makes me so ashamed ..."

He drew her closer and rested her head on his chest. "You are perfect for me, Imelda. I love you, and that is what matters."

She slept on his chest, listening to his heartbeat.

*

"I don collect am Oga," Kabiru said.

Edu grinned, collected, and played the voice recording.

"Good job, Kabiru." Edu slapped him on the back.

It hadn't been difficult to link the attempted murder case to Chinyeaka. Her sudden fondness for Ken, her disappearance from the business line—she had reappeared a few months later with a fabricated tale of a relationship with some Ken and how he had been making out with her, hoodwinking some people with it. The rumour was a huge one that he had almost believed.

"Thank you, sir. Thank you," Kabiru said, grinning.

"This will help me a lot," Edu commented, transferring the voice recording to his own phone.

The young man had made his search easier. He had stumbled on him and Chinyeaka one of the weekends he'd gone to unwind with 'the boys' and had followed him from a distance before calling him to a stop.

"Who is the girl you were speaking with?"

It had been the wrong question. Kabiru had looked him up and had left without answering.

It had taken him a week and his money to get the young man to sing like a canary. "She works at that restaurant. Her cousin stays in town. I have been doing jobs for her."

When the poisoning case had sprung up, Edu had put two and two together and known that either Kabiru had done it, or they had paid someone else to do the job. But with the testimony he had gotten, Chinyeaka had done the job herself!

"But Oga o, na true say that woman no die?" Kabiru asked with all seriousness.

Edu gave him a sharp glance. "How you did you know about this?"

"Ehm … The girl said it. I had turned off my voice recorder when she made the statement. I couldn't bring out my phone to record again. She may suspect me if I had done that."

"Jesus Christ! So how did she know … What else did she say?" Edu asked, dragging Kabiru by the hand to his car.

"I don't know, sir, but trust her now, she knows everything. I think she has been following that auntie,"

Kabiru said, his eyes darting around the interior of the car. "Oga your car fine o."

"Ehen … What else?" Edu asked.

"Oga, I don't know again. I did what you want me to do. Pay me my balance, let me bounce." He hesitated. "Okay, she has a plan. I don't know what this plan is yet o." He frowned. "But she said I will help her with the plan, sha. Since we are friends, she said this would be the last time. She wants to settle the matter once and for all …"

"And when is she planning to carry out this plan?" Edu asked.

"I don't know." He slapped the back of his hand and shrugged. "She said she will call me when she is ready."

"Now, Kabiru, you will do all you can to delay her action. Let her tell you what her plans are, and inform me of every move!" Edu pleaded.

"Oga, this thing is beginning to turn into an action movie. Me I don't like the way this whole thing is going, I no wan enter olokpa net at all. That girl can kill someone, and the police will come for me. I just want my money, so I can go …"

"Nothing will happen to you, I promise. Just keep an eye on her for me abeg," Edu continued as he brought out some Naira notes and handed them over to Kabiru.

Kabiru quickly snatched the money from him and walked away.

Edu pulled the phone from his pocket and made a call to Ken.

"She knows Grace is alive."

*

"She knows … How?"

Not every day did one get to replicate movies, but presently, it had sounded like a film brought to life, a horror one, at that. Stalking, obsession, looming murder! What was going on?

It hadn't been a thing for him when the rumour that he had slept with the girl and had promised her marriage surfaced. Any desperate lady can say anything, and fools can choose to believe whatever.

But Edu trying to convince him of something darker and sinister about the said girl—unbelievable.

He looked over his shoulder and saw Grace scooping something inside her mouth. Their eyes met, and he smiled. He had wanted this day to come, missed every moment, and had even forgotten what it felt like to share a home with a woman. Two nights ago, her panties had hung on the bathroom curtain rail.

Four years ago, he would have made a fuss about having her lingerie scattered everywhere. Now, he had learnt to appreciate the precious gift of a second chance, so he had gone to where she was, held her by the waist, and said, "Welcome home, my Grace."

"So what do we do?" he asked Edu, scratching his chin. 'Everybody is his own police in this town."

Do half of the job—and the police would take it up from where you stopped. He hissed.

"I am on her trail, but would alert a brother who is a commissioner in the police."

He strode towards the window, parted one of the curtains, and peered out. "I have turned you into a detective, my friend."

"You are a good man, Ken. I have been looking for an opportunity to pay you back for getting me back on my feet when I lost everything in that fire five years ago. And besides, I have a personal score with that girl."

"I don't know about your score, but please be careful, my friend."

"Does she know about her?" Edu asked.

"Who? Oh ..."

Ken gave Grace a quick glance. She was flipping through pages of a magazine that had been there for God knew how long, moving her head to the tune from her phone. She was happy.

He arched his brow. When they should be planning a second wedding, they were busy fighting a deranged idiot.

"Not yet. I didn't think this would happen," he replied.

"Let her know. It will be better."

CHAPTER TWENTY-EIGHT

"This is crazy. You mean a certain lady roams the street of this Lagos, desperately wanting you for herself, to the point of trying to harm those she thinks are standing in her way?"

She batted her eyelids—it was no joke. Ken would not go this far just to prove a point.

"I will want to be dropping you off to work and bringing you back myself." And that was his solution?

"For now, yes," he said.

"Ridiculous!" she muttered under her breath.

What was she supposed to do? She wasn't a child, nor was she vulnerable. Was that how he saw her?

"I don't know what is going on, Ken, but I can take care of myself." They were in the compound, at the car porch, already seated inside her car, and he wanted her to join him. She wasn't Mary, whose husband brought her to work every day.

"You are not listening to me."

"No, you are not listening!" She shut her eyes and tightened her fist. "Whatever is going on has nothing to do with me. You should have taken care of it before you brought my baby and me here."

"Whatever is going on almost got you killed! Same person we are suspecting poisoned you!" His voice had gone high.

"You are shouting!" she said, opening her eyes.

"And you are shouting!" he echoed.

Awkward silence.

Heavy breath.

They were doing it again—arguing, raising voices at each other. No, she was the one shouting. She bit her lip and looked away. Christ! Why was she getting angry?

She knew now. Once her job had been mentioned ...

"Slow down ... Take a rest ... Let me take you and bring you back ...

She felt threatened, her space invaded. It rang a bell—it was her fear. She sighed.

"Let's go inside for a minute, allow me to explain this thing to you. This is not the right place."

He had never been one for open confrontation; he hated it. She felt ashamed.

"I didn't plan to put us into this mess. I don't even know how it got to this," he said.

"How long has this been going on?" she asked.

Seated, facing him, knees touching, she allowed him to take her hands.

"For some months now. Seriously, I didn't give it any attention when it all started. I never knew it would get to this."

"You didn't tell me about this. All this time, you didn't even say anything related to this," she said softly.

It baffled her why someone would desperately want a man to this point. What had really happened between this said woman and her man? Did she have something against Ken? She didn't want to think that the two of them had something between them.

"Did you sleep with her?" she swallowed and asked, voice trembling with jealousy.

"Jesus, no! I didn't. I didn't even touch her."

She wanted to believe him or even dismiss it. It had happened before she came back to him.

"Please believe me. I had nothing intimate with her. She just wanted to ruin me, and I don't know why."

"I don't understand this. You didn't promise her love or marriage, and you didn't sleep with her. Then why is she after you? Why you, Kay?"

"That is the question I have been asking myself, too. I don't know, seriously. Now you understand why I was insisting on escorting you," he said, his hand on her cheek.

She nodded. "But you cannot follow me around forever. We have to find a way to stop this once and for all."

"Yes, babe. Edu and I are working something out. We are trying to nail her permanently. But for now, please promise me that you will be careful," he pleaded.

"I'm a mature woman."

"You are my babe. I don't want to lose you." His fingers traced down from her collarbone to her chest, then to her breast, gave her nipple a little pinch through her clothes.

"Ouch! Kay, please."

"Please what?" he asked, still playing with the hard nipple.

A few of her buttons came loose, exposing her black lace bra that now seemed small with the swelling of her breasts. Pregnancy had given her that gift.

"I have to get to work." She laughed, jerked up, and he followed.

*

The night of that same day, she lay beside him.

"Hey." He bent to meet her face.

"I thought you had slept," she said.

"You are not making it easier for me. What you are doing with my nipples?" He smiled.

Grace was thrilled.

"Should I stop?" It came with the pregnancy, maybe, or her body wanted to make up for the time they had been apart. "I seem to desire you every day. I can't set my eyes on you without thinking of sex."

He was massaging her scalp, the way that turned her on.

"I am hot." He chuckled. "You have never been able to resist me since I've known you."

She slapped his chest, and he pinned her hand to his hairy, toned pecs. Life should be like this—laying and waking up every day in the arms of the person you loved. She heaved a sigh.

"Kay, I can't sleep."

"Hmm … Okay." He tightened his arm around her. "Here, let me hold you. I will try not to do more than that," he whispered in her ear.

"But I have something else in mind."

She slid her flimsy pink nightwear off. Her hard nipples throbbed against him. She ran her hand on his body while he lay still, drew closer, caressed his face, slipped a finger in his mouth, and ran it over his tongue.

"Hmm." He sucked on her finger.

She replaced it with her tongue, ran it around his lips before slipping inside his mouth. She wanted him so much.

"You are a seductress, you know that?" His voice filled with lust as he slapped her backside.

"You said I can't resist you." She gave his lips a bite. "Let's see who can't resist who now."

She left his neck and covered his nipple with her mouth while caressing his hard erection.

"Oh, God!" he moaned.

He threw his hands on her head and pushed her downward. She understood what he wanted. Her lips found it—her tongue explored the shaft, forming a ring at the top. She teased him, toyed with his arousal, wetting it. She played with his balls before she took him in her mouth.

"Grace ..."

"Hmm," she moaned as she felt her wetness, a hot flush like the bloom of the flowering season. He held her head and thrust, lifting her head and bringing it back.

She slowly pulled away and crawled on top of him, eyes fixed on his squinted eyes. She leaned on his chest and whispered in his ear.

"What do you want, Kay?" she said in a gravelly purr.

"Just don't stop ..."

That night, she was his temptress, his sex queen, his seductress, and his woman in all senses. She looked him in the eyes as she rode him, slowing down at intervals to allow him to calm down. She was in control, and he loved it.

He held her butt cheeks with his hands, and she thrilled him with the feel of her buttocks bouncing up and down. There was nothing calm and quiet about the woman on top of him—she was taking him to the world of ecstasy.

Her muscles contracted, her tempo changed, the ride got faster, and her eyes widened. A loud moaner, she couldn't hold back as spasms shook her body. He let himself go, holding her hips firmly as he thrust inside her faster.

His orgasm came as well as hers. With a loud moan, he gave the last thrust and was still, holding her as she shook vigorously from her climax.

She laid on his chest, planting kisses on his face and upper body. Exhausted, but fulfilled, she didn't wish to be anywhere but in his arms.

"This is the woman I married," he said, caressing her. "Thank you so much, sweet."

He kissed her as she lay beside him.

*

They say to get something done, one had to do it himself—and that was what Chinyeaka planned to do. Only that she needed to know where the woman was. She wouldn't want to spill blood in Ken's house. That would be a bad omen. Her blood would haunt the house and disrupt the peace she was planning to have with her man.

Palm covering her jaw and part of her mouth, she tapped her fingers on the bridge of her nose. It should be somewhere else. Somewhere discreet.

That was where Kabiru came in. That he-goat, mkpi ofia! That had resorted to blackmailing her for free fuck and more money. She wished she could do away with him, as well, but she was not a murderer. This was a necessity and would be the only one she would do.

She looked down at the two-edged blade she'd purchased from the store. It wasn't tricky buying it as nobody asked why anyone would buy a knife in the market.

Unlike the poison, there would be no mistake this time as she would be the person that would thrust the blade inside her heart. She would watch her bleed and would amuse herself when she would open her bloodless mouth to scream with no words coming out. She would watch her turn white.

She would be her death.

CHAPTER TWENTY-NINE

Grace searched for the bunch of keys hidden amidst the pile of papers scattered on her desk. It had been two months since she had been discharged from the hospital and had not been to her house. How ridiculous it now sounded to refer to it as 'her house,' yet she needed to get her things out.

She wouldn't even bring it up with Ken, knowing what his response would be.

"We have to be careful. Please avoid that place for now, until we unravel this case," he would say.

Two months and nothing had happened to her. They had even stopped discussing it.

"I think I will be going to my house after work," she said to Mary.

"You still have a house? The one now occupied by rats and roaches," Mary commented.

"That's none your business." She hunched over her desk. "My things are still there, and my rent has not expired."

She didn't know if anyone would understand. She didn't miss being alone. Ken had been all loving and caring. She wouldn't wish for anything else better in this world. But she secretly craved for the power the house gave her. It shamed her to say it. Allowing herself to be taken care of would take a little getting used to.

"Anyway, please don't let Ken know I am going there." She found the key, threw it in the air, and caught it mid-way.

"Come o, Grace. Why shouldn't I let your husband know where you are going to?" Mary gave her a suspicious look.

"Get away, you. What do you think I am going there to do? I just want to get a few things and bid farewell to the house." Grace laughed and sat down. "Ken insisted that it is not safe yet. For all he knows, whoever it was that wanted me dead may still be trailing me."

"And I agree with him, girlfriend. Please be careful. I think you shouldn't go there now. One needs to be safe, you know."

"For how long? For how long, Mary? How can I be hiding from someone I don't know? This person may have left the state knowing that the police are after her."

"You are very stubborn. I don't even know how Ken deals with you!" Mary sneered. "Give this thing time. There is nothing in that house you cannot buy anew."

"I know, Mary." She exhaled "But I just want to be there … You will not really understand."

"Hmm. Okay o, but I am scared. I don't want to cry. I don't even have a black dress to wear for your funeral," Mary joked.

"God forbid! Tufiakwa!" Grace made a circle over her head with her fingers and snapped them as if throwing away a bad omen.

Mary laughed and playfully slapped her arm. "I was only joking, girlfriend. Don't take it seriously."

"Who jokes with death?" Grace warned. "Please don't get me scared. Nothing will happen to me. I have already weathered the storm. This is nothing."

"Anyways, how is Imelda?" Mary relaxed her back on the chair.

"She is fine. Her fine ass lover got her a business," Grace said with a smile.

"Really! Wow, I am so happy for her. What does she sell?"

"She now sells Abada and lace materials. You really need to be there."

"Eehee! Na big business o, see Imelda has become her own boss, I am here running errands for this ungrateful man," Mary lamented.

"I bought one beautiful Indian George from her last Saturday. You really have to visit the place o. She stocked her shop with beautiful and attractive materials."

"That is good for her, at least. That Ahmad of a guy is no longer in her life. This new guy seems promising."

"He adores her."

*

Chinyeaka made up her mind for the third time that day. She would not rely on Kabiru for information. He had been acting weird lately, placing outrageous demands.

"This thing would be done on my terms when I am ready to do it," he had said.

She knew he was up to something. First, it was an increase in what she used to give him. "The money is too small for what you want me to do for you. Do you know what it means to follow people around without being caught? Maybe you should come and do it yourself."

Then he had asked for 'fucks' whenever she couldn't come up with any money. "I have seen you gave it to those your customers in their cars. What difference does it make?"

Ugly baboon with rotten teeth.

Then he had stopped coming, stopped picking her calls even, had not asked her for money lately, and that was a relief and a cause to worry, too. He was a wretched street boy who should always require cash and free pussy. That was how she'd met him—hungry. She had what he wanted and wouldn't give it to him until he had earned it.

She checked the plates. Her madam had warned her about serving costumers food with dishes that had stains. She picked the ceramic soup plate with her trembling hands. It slipped from her fingers and smashed into many pieces on the hard floor.

"Mtchewwww," she hissed. It was becoming a habit. Looking through the door to make sure nobody was in view, she hurriedly swept the broken pieces and threw them in the dustbin. This would be the second plate she was breaking.

Her palms sweaty and her heart beating faster, she heaved a sigh to steady her trembling bones. She had planned to end it all today. She knew where she worked, and when she closed from work. If she was lucky, she would follow her—no plans of where it would be.

"How will you do that? What if her husband is at home?" Kabiru had asked.

"Don't call him that. He is not her husband. I am the only woman qualified to be called his wife," she had warned him.

Kabiru had been drinking pepper soup in their restaurant that evening. That had been before he stopped coming around.

"No vex. Oya, tell me, how you wan take follow am?" he had asked again.

"You shouldn't concern yourself with how I would get it done. I have planned it since. Oga Ken goes to church every Wednesday. He doesn't miss it."

She had considered doing it at the gate before, but there were many things wrong with that plan.

She had to do this anyway—there was no going back. A sacrifice worth paying for love.

*

Nothing had changed from the last time she had been there, except for the strong, musty smell and the ceiling that had caved a little. The sitting room was still in disarray, one of the dining chairs overturned.

The kitchen was no better when she wandered into it, leftover food turned into worm larvae incubator. She was tempted to clean the kitchen, decided against it, didn't think she was up to the job.

She veered towards her bedroom, collapsed on her bed, and heaved a sigh. Her gaze rove around her unkempt bed and settled on her laptop. She grabbed it and clutched it to her chest, then she heard her gate open. Startled, she headed towards the window and peered, waited to hear footsteps of someone calling her name. Okay, this house held an unpleasant memory. She peered again. Must be the wind.

Darkness was fast closing on the sky, and she needed to gather her few things hurriedly before Ken came back and started looking for her.

The noise came again, this time inside the house, the sound of a door opening and closing. She was beginning to get scared and peered through the dining. Her gaze travelled through the sitting room, but she saw nothing.

She went back inside the room, brought down her box, and started shoving some clothes inside.

*

It hadn't been easy for Chinyeaka to convince the keke driver to follow the car until she'd grudgingly handed him three thousand Naira. The woman had taken another turn that led to her former house. Eyes widened, she'd urged the driver to follow. Wasn't life playing in her favour? The silly woman had already chosen her own venue of death.

"Madam, abeg come down we done reach."

The keke driver snapped her out from her thoughts.

She cleaned her sweaty palms on her trousers. With her dagger hiding inside her handbag, she stepped out.

The gate flinched at her push—she had actually been expecting some resistance. Adjusting her dark shades and pulling a hood over her head, she walked into the compound, stumbled on the gate crossing, and staggered, knocking off the glasses from her face. She regained her balance, looked over her shoulder, her pulse quickening.

I am here. It must be done.

She saw her when the woman peered through the window. She was already in the house when she moved a heavy object, and when Grace was done with packing, Chinyeaka was waiting.

*

"Hello, Oga Edu … Elo, elllоооо!" Kabiru screamed from the phone.

"Hello, Kabiru, thank God! I have been trying to get you, but no avail," Edu replied.

"No thank God o, your girl said she will follow that Oga Ken madam go house o," Kabiru said.

"I don't understand. Follow her go house how?" Edu asked.

"I don't know. I just told you what I heard. I think she has something terrible in mind. Me, I have washed my hands off this thing."

"Are you serious?"

"No, I no serious, see this man o, I am telling you so you can do something. You are here asking me if I am serious," Kabiru rebuked and cut the call.

Edu dialled Ken's number twice. He wanted to hang up after the third try, but Ken picked up.

"Where is Grace?" was the first thing he asked.

"She should be in the house. Why are you asking?"

"We have a serious problem at hand. Please leave wherever you are and start going home."

"What is the problem? Is she in any form of trouble?"

"Nwokem ajuzinam ajuju ahu, don't ask me that question now. Start going home now. I am on my way."

Edu entered his car and drove off.

CHAPTER THIRTY

She wasn't alone.

Grace could no longer ignore the sense of foreboding that enveloped her. She'd always had that hunch when something wrong was about to happen to her or someone around her, like when her father died in a plane crash. That day she was poisoned—she had felt that chill and goosebumps, though it had disappeared as soon as it had come.

This one wasn't disappearing. It got more substantial like a shadow hanging over her head in the dark. The hairs on her nape and arms rose. The cracking of her door made her turn with a start. She wheezed out air, clutching her heart. Christ!

No one there.

That door! Always making that silly cracky noise.

She walked to the door and closed it properly, then went back to packing, brought down her suits and fitted gowns.

"I will not be using them for a long while until this baby is born," she muttered, but still, she packed them in the box.

She brought out the gown she had worn to the birthday party and which had led to her pregnancy.

"You and I have a long business together," she said and carefully folded it inside the box while rubbing her protruding stomach with her left hand and smiling.

The door cracked again, but since she had gotten used to it, she paid it no heed.

*

Imelda got down from the taxi.

"Abeg, wait for me. I only have a few things to pick from this house." She gestured towards the apartment.

Staying with Kola was a blessing. A gift she didn't know would come her way. All she needed was to pick her remaining things from this house—give Grace a call, hoping she would pick up this time.

She was astounded when she didn't find the gate padlocked. She pushed, and it squeaked open. Who else could have opened the house if not Grace? If she was inside, then that would be better.

*

Chinyeaka banged the door as she walked in, deliberately announcing her presence. The torch from the woman's phone provided the only light in the room. Good. She wouldn't want her to see her shaky limbs.

The woman turned sharply to the sound of the door shutting behind her and came face to face with her fear—Chinyeaka. Her eyes went down her thick jumpsuit and worn-out boots.

She pulled down her hood and allowed her to see her low-tinted hair.

"Finally, this is you," she said, hands inside her pockets.

Chinyeaka stared at the woman for a while, and bile rose to her throat. She sought the weapon. With her eyes still fixed on the woman, she brought it out and discarded the bag.

"Jesus!" the woman shouted, stepping backwards.

"You shout Jesus? You think He is here to save you?" She balanced her grip on the knife. "Oh, I see. You don't want to die. Na today I go know say whether you be ghost abi human being."

Enjoying the fear she saw in the other woman's eyes, Chinyeaka moved forward, wielding the blade.

The buzzing of the woman's phone disrupted the moment. Grace made to pick it up.

"Don't you even think about it! No try am, no even look the phone!" she warned.

When the phone rang again, both women looked at each other, waiting, calculating. The phone rang continuously until Chinyeaka switched it off and threw it inside her pocket.

"I know you don't know me, but I know you very well. I have been following you for a very long time. You have been enjoying life with my man, strolling this street, parading yourself now. I heard you left him before," she said, the weapon lowering a little.

*

This must be her.

Grace's eyes widened. This was the woman. Why? She was just a girl. She couldn't see clearly, but she knew the girl before her wouldn't be more than twenty-three!

What should she do? She could launch at her, but the knife ... What if she had backups waiting outside?

"... I have tried to make Oga Ken love me. Each time it seems the relationship was about to work, you will show up ... destroying everything I have built." The girl tilted her head sideways and cast her gaze on Grace's stomach, smirked. "You even got pregnant, so you can trap him."

Grace didn't miss the tremor in her voice. She was also scared.

"Since you are the only thing preventing Oga Ken from taking me seriously, I am going to send both you and that bastard baby to Hellfire," she said, then strode towards Grace and pushed her onto the bed.

"You don't have to do this. Please, I am begging you. Don't do this. For the sake of God, please ..." Grace pleaded.

"Shut up, you old woman." The girl looked over her shoulder, back to her. "Why didn't you disappear when you had the chance?" The dagger now pressed against her neck. "You left him. You should have never come back! You have a good job, you have money, what else do you want?" she screamed.

"Please, I am begging you for the sake of my baby. Please let me go ..." Grace pleaded again.

"Which baby? This one?" The blade left her neck for her stomach. "You know how many times I begged him to sleep with me, to let me carry his baby? And he turned me down? What makes you think I will spare you because of this protruding stomach?"

The girl sneered. One knee firmly on the floor, the other pressed Grace's legs against the bed while her fingers tightened around her neck. She was more powerful than Grace had thought.

"Please don't do this to me ... Don't do this to yourself. You are a beautiful lady. Any man would want to have you ..." she said in a painful rasp—she could hardly breathe. Eyes bulging, she threw her fists on the girl.

"Any man, you say? I don't need any man. I need Oga Ken. Unfortunately, killing you is the only way to set him free."

*

"Hello! Is anybody in?" Imelda called.

Walking into a chair, she winced, sat down on the floor, and massaged the hurting foot. How could anyone be in this house without light? She cursed under her breath, groped inside her bag for her phone, and managed to turn the torch on.

"What happened here?" she muttered slowly as her gaze roved with her beam. She had not been to the house after the night of the incident.

"Hello … Grace, are you upstairs?"

She got to her feet, hopped a little before balancing her weight on the hurting leg. Grace's car was outside, so she should be inside.

But something didn't sit right. Grace wasn't one to be careless with security. Not after an attempt on her life.

"Grace, are you here?" she called out again and headed towards the room.

*

Chinyeaka made a sharp move, launched towards the intruder—dragged her inside and barricaded the door with her body. Teeth bared, chest rising and falling with heavy breath, legs widened, she kept the person pinned on the ground. She hadn't planned to have two women there. She trembled inside, eyes darting from one woman to another.

Her plans would not be ruined. Too bad this other woman had joined. She would have to kill both of them and bolt before another person entered the party. She had to clean the mess.

"What the …" The newcomer looked from Grace on the bed to Chinyeaka by the door. "What is going on here?"

"Don't come closer … I am warning you!" Chinyeaka gripped the weapon tight, swerving side to side, face covered in perspiration.

"You!" the new woman exclaimed. "I know you!"

She threw her a glare.

"Oya, join your friend, no be me do you, na you wan die come carry your two left legs come here when nobody invite you" Chinyeaka ordered, gesturing with her knife. "Join her!"

"It's you! The girl that brought the wine the other day!" the woman said, stepping backwards.

Fear gripped her. It would have been easy if she had been dealing with only one woman.

"I said you should join your friend—"

Chinyeaka hadn't finished when the new woman charged, knocking the dagger off her hand. It landed on the floor beside the wardrobe.

Grace went for it at the same time she did. Pushing her off, Chinyeaka had dived before the pregnant woman, got the knife first while Grace gripped her hand.

A fight ensued, both women struggling. Chinyeaka freed her hand, pushed Grace against the wall. She landed with her shoulder, lost her balance, and crumbled on the floor.

The other woman jumped on her back, held her hands together. Chinyeaka shoved her with her elbow. Filled with rage and fear, she blindly flung the blade round. The woman screamed at the sight of her own blood.

With the knife lifted above her head, Chinyeaka walked towards Grace, teeth bared, eyes fixed on her target—she made a move.

The first stroke caught her by the shoulder. She could feel her nerves give way as the knife drove its way deep inside her.

Grace screamed, crawled backwards while holding her bleeding shoulder. She saw the warm fluid soak her back, her clothes, and run down her body.

The blood excited Chinyeaka. Nothing would make her happier than to torment this woman that had tortured her soul for long. She was fast, pulled the dagger out of the shoulder. Grace screamed and wriggled in pain.

She took a deep breath to stab her again …

*

He got in just in time to stop the second stab, which would have ended it all.

Ken threw his weight on Chinyeaka who held the knife above her head to strike again. Both landed on the floor, the dagger flying out of her hand.

"You don't mess with my woman!"

He pinned her to the ground, and she shrilled, struggling to free herself.

"I have had enough of your madness." He slapped the back of her head.

"Enough now, Mr Kenneth."

Edu came in with two police officers.

CHAPTER THIRTY-ONE

"Oh, sweetheart." He kissed her palm. "How many times will you do this to me?"

He bent and kissed her forehead.

Grace's lips widened in a slow smile.

"Kay," she muttered weakly and tightened her grip on his hand. "I was so scared yesterday … I thought I was going to die."

Tears trickled down her face.

He bent over her and kissed her lips passionately.

"You stubborn woman." He kissed her again, trying not to lean on her bandaged shoulder. "How did you think I would have allowed that to happen?"

She reached out and touched his face. "You look terrible."

She chuckled while he gently wiped her tears.

"Same as you."

They both laughed.

She heaved. "How did you know?"

"Mary. When Edu tipped me over the phone, I had to rush back home." He clasped her hands in his. "Imagine what went through my mind when I didn't see you at home, and you weren't picking your calls. My next option was to call Mary. She said you left some hours ago. I went mad when she told me where to find you! Why are you like this, my love? Why are you doing this to me?"

Her brow wrinkled.

"I am sorry, Kay. I only wanted to …" She had no explanation "Kay, I am so sorry. I should have listened to you."

She tried to pull herself up, grimaced.

The door swung open, and the doctor walked in, beamed the couple a smile before he adjusted the drip.

"She lost a lot of blood, but she is going to be alright." He scribbled something on a file. "Ma'am Grace, you are one tough woman."

Ken stared at her and smiled in satisfaction. "And the baby?"

"He is a hard one, so determined to live. He is fine," Doctor Ayo said with a smile.

"Doctor, you said 'he'?" Ken asked.

"Yes, Ken. You are going to have a son."

His gaze rested on her face as the doctor left. They'd had their differences, had argued and fought, but he cherished and adored this woman. Now they were going to have a child! A dream come true.

"I love you so much, my little woman."

"I have made you go through so much, Kay."

"You have made me a happy and fulfilled man." He touched her lips. "A new beginning. A second chance is what we have, sweetheart."

"Kay." Her heart pulsated. "You are everything I have ever wanted. I didn't see it then, but I am ready to start this new beginning with you, my husband."

"Husband … I like the sound of that."

EPILOGUE

"You are looking radiant."

"Thank you, Mama."

She was getting ready for her wedding—the second wedding, actually. It was all Ken's idea. She couldn't believe it when he'd walked into the hospital after her mother had left.

"Kay—"

"Grace—"

They had both started and had laughed.

"You first," he'd said to her.

"Kay, I have reflected on everything that happened, and ... I am ready to open my heart to making a perfect family with you. I was blinded by my selfishness. You told me we could work this out without losing who we are. I agree with you." He had nodded with a grin. "I may not know how to do all those wifey things, but ... I am ready to learn."

"Shhhhhhh." He had placed his fingers on her lips. "You are enough for me, my little woman. I don't want a strong woman. I want my Grace. She may be a little stubborn, but let her be willing to listen to me, too, and agree sometimes."

They had laughed.

"I want to share your life with you. I want to make decisions with you, and I want to be allowed to love you properly," he continued.

"Then you have me, all of me. You are the only man I have loved, and I still love you like mad. You mean so much to me."

He held her gaze while fishing something out of his pocket. When he held it up, she saw what it was and gasped.

"It's nothing fancy," he said. "It doesn't equate to how much I love and want to be with you again. Since you have agreed to come back, I think, well, we should make it official again."

"Ken ..."

"Marry me again, sweet." He had opened the little box, exposing a simple but beautiful gold ring. "We can get a priest here now to do it for us or any time you want."

He'd smiled, removing her old ring and slipping the new one on her finger as tears filled her eyes.

"I have loved you from the beginning, never stopped loving you all these years. I want to make sure you are not running off again."

Her lips had quivered.

"Please," Ken had added. "Marry me, my love."

Please? He was begging her?

"What is wrong with you? I am your wife already."

"We were divorced, remember? Besides, I want to start anew. This will be a new beginning for us. We have to retake our vows. That is if you agree to marry me again," he had said.

"Of course, I want that very much." She had sniffled. No fear, nor worry—she knew it would be different this time. With him helping her, she would be the wife and the mother he had always wanted her to be.

"I love you so much, sweet," he'd said while stroking her hair.

"I love you, too, Kay."

A few weeks later, they were ready to march to the altar to take their vows for the second and last time.

"I knew both of you would come back together," her mother-in-law said to her, drawing her back.

She smiled. They were in her room, with Imelda, her bridesmaid, and Mary, who were putting some finishing touches on her face and her hair.

"I thought we were over, Mama. This is a miracle."

"Both of you are meant for each other. You were eager to walk away and didn't see reasons to right the wrongs that led to your marriage breaking down."

"It was my fault, Mama. Ken has been good to me."

"No, my child. Ken has his own fault, too. Maybe he also let go easily."

"I know better now, Mama. I will never allow us to break down again," Grace assured her.

"Don't worry, Mama. I will keep an eye on her and will reset her brain for her whenever she starts to misbehave," Mary chipped in, and they all laughed.

"I don't think there will be any need for that again. My daughter-in-law has learnt from the past," her mother-in-law said as she stood up to leave. "It is almost time to go get my husband from the airport. I hope we get back in time before you guys leave for church."

"Your eyes still sparkle whenever you talk about Chief," Grace teased.

"Of course. He is my husband, and I still love him so much," the older woman said with a blush before she left.

"I hope I will be able to talk about Ken like that after many years," Grace commented.

"Of course you will. Ken is a lovely guy, and don't forget, like father, like son," Mary said, blowing off some excess powder from the brush.

"She is so nice. If my mother-in-law was to be alive, she would have been as nice as her," Imelda said dreamingly.

"Eh!" echoed Grace and Mary.

"What?' Imelda feigned ignorance.

"That reminds me, I have been ignoring this shiny stone on your ring finger since today. Does it have anything to do with your sudden mother-in-law talk?" Mary asked, with her hands akimbo.

"Yes, tell us, Imelda. My ears are itching for good news."

"We are here for your wedding—"

"Second wedding, don't forget," Mary corrected.

"Okay, second wedding, so let's concentrate on that. We will talk about me later," Imelda said and brought down the wedding gown from the wardrobe.

"Let us hear it ..." Mary said.

"There is still time," Grace added.

"Okay, ehm, he proposed," Imelda said with a smile.

The two ladies squealed. Mary hugged Imelda, lifted her from the ground, and spun her around. Grace clapped.

"But who proposed?" Mary asked.

The other two women looked at her with surprise.

"Kolawole!" Grace said.

"Our super chef?" Mary asked.

"Yes," Imelda replied.

"Oh my goodness, that is a good and handsome baby bear you got for yourself. I saw the way he was running around all the while you were detained. Wow, girlfriend, you have done it this time," Mary said.

"Thank you so much, Mary."

Imelda then fastened the hooks on the wedding gown and tightened the knot, brushed the hem.

"Oh, such a sexy man, with some cheeks and stomach. You don't need another pillow to lay your head ..." Mary continued.

"Mary!" Grace shouted, stopping her friend from going further.

"I was only admiring God's creature."

"Admire your husband."

"Wow, your wedding gown is beautiful. You look so amazing," Imelda said and clamped her hands on her cheeks, her eyelids fluttering.

"Thank you, dear. I owe a lot to you. You made me see and appreciate love, and you somehow made this possible," Grace said to her.

"What about me?" Mary asked.

"You try sha."

The three of them burst into laughter.

Two soft knocks and her husband walked in, already dressed.

"And here comes the groom," Imelda muttered, dragging Mary as they left the room.

Ken waited for the door to close before he pulled her into his arms and kissed her passionately.

"You have ruined my lipstick," she said, cleaning off the lipstick stain from his lips.

"They will help you with another one," Ken replied.

"It's a taboo to see the bride before the wedding," she joked.

"Says who?"

"I don't know."

They both laughed.

"You look amazing." She admired her husband.

"And you, my wife, are beautiful."

"No, my curve is gone. My stomach is big," she said and looked down at her belly.

"Maybe I am beginning to have a new fantasy, making love to a pregnant woman in a wedding gown." He lifted her face to his. "You are sexy even with the pregnancy."

"Are you sure?"

"I am very sure, and can't wait to have you all to myself after the wedding. I want to make love to you until both of us are breathless."

"Stop doing this to me. You are getting me wet," she admitted.

"Then let's have a quick one before we go out there," he suggested.

"You are crazy. It's not proper," she said, hitting him on the chest and laughing, but lust nevertheless coursed through her.

"Nothing is proper when it comes to my desire towards you."

They were about to kiss again when they heard voices, laughter, and footsteps.

"My father is here, and I heard your brother is here, too."

"What about my mum?" she asked.

"She is giving the caterers a tough time."

"Typical of my mother. Let us go and meet Chief."

He helped her up, and she slipped her feet inside the silver block heel sandals, then both of them walked out hand in hand.

In his room, inside his suitcase, lay two flight tickets to the Bahamas, sponsored by Morgan and a letter to Grace.

He would surprise her with that after the wedding.

Thank you for reading One More Night by Rosemary Okafor. If you enjoyed this story, please leave a review on the site of purchase.

Continue reading for Chapter One excerpt from When Love Happens by Rosemary Okafor featured in the Be My Valentine Anthology: Volume Two.

Morgan is ruthless and plays dirty to protect his billion-dollar conglomerate. However, he holds a dark secret that could destroy him if exposed. His relationships with women are about pleasure alone until one weekend with the beautiful Eno leaves him ready to risk everything for her. Eno was a young journalist when she witnessed Morgan murder his wife. Six years later, she's ready to do anything to make him pay for his crime. Until she falls for his charms. Now she's torn between destroying the proud billionaire and allowing herself to fall in-love with him.

WHEN LOVE HAPPENS

BY

ROSEMARY OKAFOR

CHAPTER ONE

"Are you ready for this?"

Eno adjusted her headset and muttered gibberish into her mic.

"Can you reduce the volume a bit?"

This would be the second time she would be seeing the Abuja business mogul. The first time had been six years ago at Sheraton Hotel—she was starting her career as a journalist and had gone to Abuja with her boss to see him about the murder of his wife.

"Say something. Let me take your level," Eric, her camera man, instructed. "Okay ... perfect." He confirmed with a thumb up.

No matter how long she had done this, interviews like this made her nervous.

"It is not every day one gets to interview Chief Morgan Cookey." Eric threw her a glance with an encouraging smile.

"I know, Eric." She ran her fingers on her dreadlocks plaited into a Mohawk and adjusted her glasses closer to her eyes. "I just don't know what to expect ... It is difficult to know which question is appropriate."

The hot weather was beginning to grease her T-zone, making her glasses too heavy for her small nose to carry. She removed them again and wiped her nose with her palm before replacing them. The thing balanced better on top of the bridge, and she wiped her sweaty palms on her dress.

"It is no different from interviewing Dangote and Otedola. This is your beat, Eno. Why are you nervous?"

"I have met this man before. Believe me, he is different from the two you just mentioned. He is a monster."

"How did you figure that out? Have you spoken to him before?" He glanced at her again, bemused. "Okay, you actually have to calm down. You are practically freaking out. You will be fine"

"Really? I mean ... is it that obvious?" She pointed at her face.

Eric dabbed his hankie on her face. "The meeting will soon be over, and he will be out any moment. I wouldn't want you to ruin my video."

"Thank you, Eric."

The pandemonium around them announced his emergence. Journalists straightened themselves, arranged their gadgets, and pushed their way forward as the door to the prestigious Presidential Hotel Reception flew open and heavily armed men swam out first before he stepped out between them.

None of them had planned for the silence that followed his emergence. To Eno, his aura was still as intimidating as it had been twelve years ago. The only time she had felt that aura was six years ago when she was in Lagos to interview '*Charlie Boy.*'

Chief Morgan cleared his throat and flashed one of the most amazing smiles she had ever seen before the *click clicks* of the cameras came alive.

"Proud bastard," she muttered. He was a handsome man, with a demeanour that was nothing but ruthless.

"He is good. It's like he was born for the camera," Eric added.

"Chief, what is the fate of the Baran Rafi community dwellers whose lands have been taken for the construction of your mega headquarter?" She broke the silence, emphasized '*your.*'

He turned and rested his gaze on her—the most intense look she had received. His eyes scrutinized her for a few seconds before he smiled.

"Wilson's Group is a company that is people-oriented. The wellbeing of the people is our concern, and we will make sure the organization improves the lives of citizens at all cost," he replied.

"But is the organization ready to dialogue with the community concerning their lands which was taken from them?" she continued.

He gave her another long look.

"I don't know about 'taking' any land. The community was well consulted before we started construction on the land, but rest assured that we are going to meet with the aggrieved faction of members to settle the matter amicably," he answered, giving her a knowing glance before he continued. "We are not the enemy of the community. We have done so much when it comes to development both in Abuja and other places. Our work speaks for us in Lagos and Enugu."

"How long are we going to wait for your company to fix a meeting with the aggrieved members of the Baran Rafi community? From the information we gathered, they said they have not received any news nor any compensation from your organization," another journalist added.

"Like I said earlier, there is a faction that feels they deserve more." He chuckled, his rich, curly beard giving his face a formidable look. "You know Nigeria. One cannot please them all."

He gave a quick glace towards where she stood. "The issue of compensation was settled two months ago. However, we will continue to foster peaceful coexistence. We will sit with the aggrieved members."

"He is good ... very good at masking his true self," Eric whispered to her.

"Hmm," she agreed.

"I have to retire now, gentlemen of the press ..." he was saying.

"How are you coping with the vacuum left by your late wife, and are we expecting a wedding soon?" she asked before she could stop herself.

Chief Morgan turned to her sharply, squinted up at her, and mockingly asked, "Are you applying to fill the vacuum?"

This evoked laughter from the crowd.

"It has been a long day," he added in finality before he tore his eyes away from her and hurried down into his car.

"That was spontaneous," Eric said while folding the cords.

She gave out a wheezing breath she hadn't known she'd been holding since Morgan had given her the sharp gaze. "Let's get back to the office."

***

"Such a nerve," Morgan muttered.

"Yes, sir. I couldn't believe Alhaji Mumuni would look you in the face and ask for an increase after what was agreed. Maybe he feels you are young and can be pushed around."

"Hmm ..." He agreed with his driver who had become family even when his father, Chief Sese Cookey, had still been alive. He was a good man who'd served his father for fifteen years and had remained with him twenty-one years after.

But he wasn't thinking about the meeting he'd had earlier, nor the swarm of media people that fought to devour him. But the young journalist ... he was sure he had seen her somewhere.

"That lady journalist. She is a fearless one," he said with a chuckle.

"Yes, sir. Too fearless for her own good."

And it fascinated him. In fact, he had been drawn to her the moment she'd asked the first question. He knew how intimidating his presence could be. He had been told about that often, but the lady hadn't been shaken by this.

This would be the first time he'd ever taken a long, interested glace at a woman after the death of Fatimah six years ago.

"Ah! Fatimah," he muttered.

She had been his world, the only woman who'd understood him perfectly. Theirs had been love at first sight, her boldness and her intelligence drawing him to her.

"What man blushes like a woman ... you are turning red!" she had commented the first day he'd met her at the hospital in Amsterdam. She was the daughter of the then-minister for works and on her annual routine medical check-up while he had visited a doctor friend.

They'd ended up becoming friends from that day and had graduated to lovers few months after. It hadn't been difficult for her to accept his proposal even though he was a Christian.

Then the fights had come.

"You are never around, Morgan. What do I do with myself?" Fatimah would cry out.

The female journalist reminded him of her. Her last question had brought back the guilt and the pains he had tried to hide. Yet, there remained something striking about her.

"I like her," he said.

"Sir?"

"The female journalist. She seems … interesting in some kind of annoying way."

His driver looked at him through the rear-view mirror. "You have not talked about liking a woman after Fatimah."

"I can't talk about any woman the way I talk about Fatimah."

"It's been six years, sir. I am sorry, sir. I shouldn't remind you—"

"Set up an appointment with her at my office," he cut in, then picked the newspaper beside him. "I will give her all the interviews she wants."

He had a mischievous smile while he turned the pages of the paper—relationships with women had become flings after the death of his wife. But maybe things were about to change.

OTHER BOOKS BY LOVE AFRICA PRESS

Not Just Another Interlude by Lara T Kareem
Fine Maple by Emem Bassey
A Little Bit of Love's Magic by Bambo Deen
Duke by Kiru Taye

CONNECT WITH US

Facebook.com/LoveAfricaPress
Twitter.com/LoveAfricaPress
Instagram.com/LoveAfricaPress

SIGN UP TO OUR NEWSLETTER
https://www.loveafricapress.com/newsletter

LOVE AFRICA PRESS
African Love Stories

www.ingramcontent.com/pod-product-compliance
Lightning Source LLC
Chambersburg PA
CBHW020815190726
48285CB00006B/2291
* 9 7 8 1 9 1 4 2 2 6 0 2 1 *